FRUIT NINJA™

FRENZY FORCE

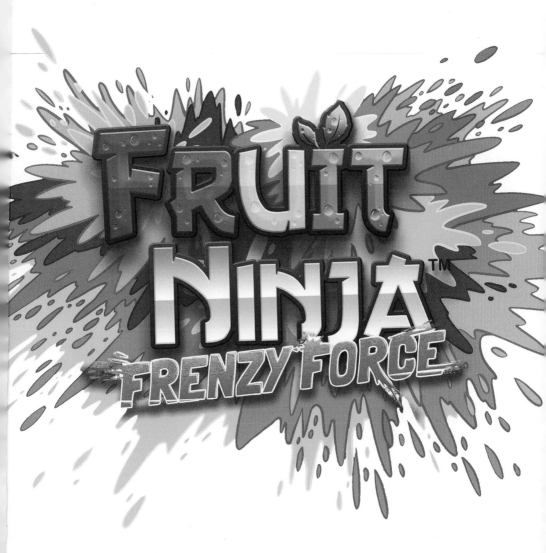

FRUIT NINJA™ FRENZY FORCE

BASED ON A SCREENPLAY BY
BRENDAN DEBOY

ADAPTED AND ILLUSTRATED BY
ERICH OWEN

Andrews McMeel
PUBLISHING®

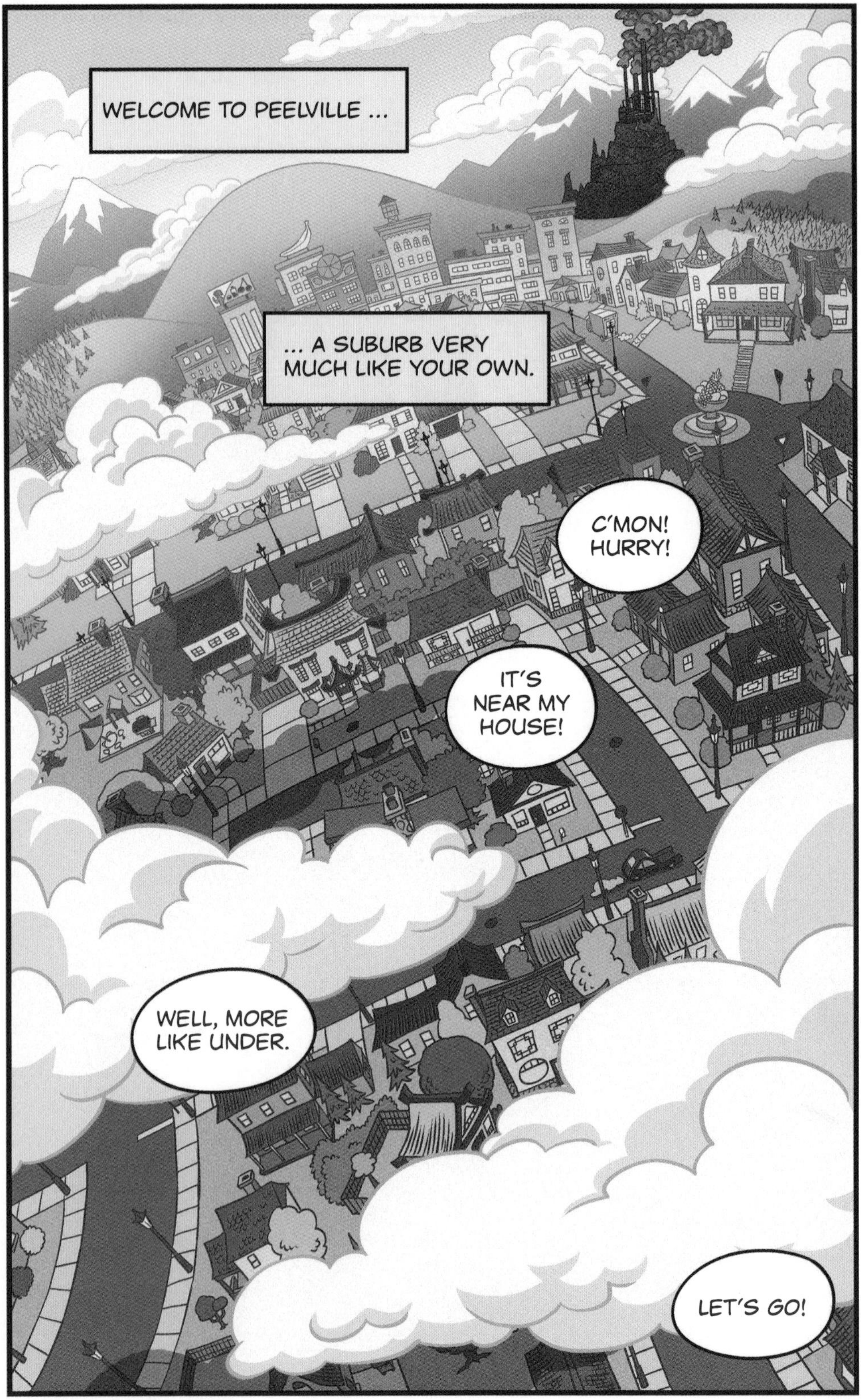
WELCOME TO PEELVILLE ...
... A SUBURB VERY MUCH LIKE YOUR OWN.
C'MON! HURRY!
IT'S NEAR MY HOUSE!
WELL, MORE LIKE UNDER.
LET'S GO!

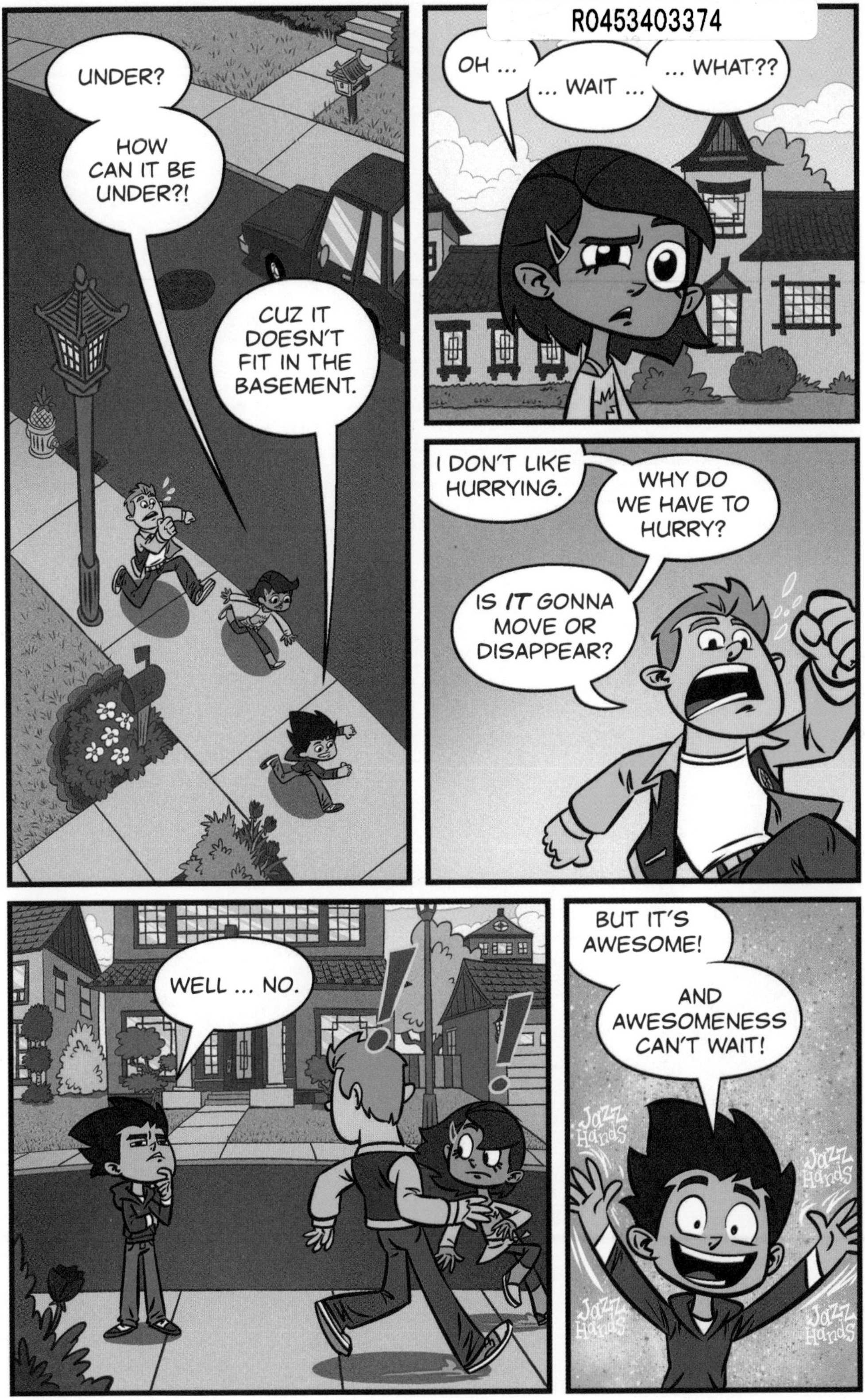
UNDER?
HOW CAN IT BE UNDER?!
CUZ IT DOESN'T FIT IN THE BASEMENT.
OH ...
... WAIT ...
... WHAT??
I DON'T LIKE HURRYING.
WHY DO WE HAVE TO HURRY?
IS *IT* GONNA MOVE OR DISAPPEAR?
WELL ... NO.
BUT IT'S AWESOME!
AND AWESOMENESS CAN'T WAIT!
Jazz Hands
Jazz Hands
Jazz Hands
Jazz Hands

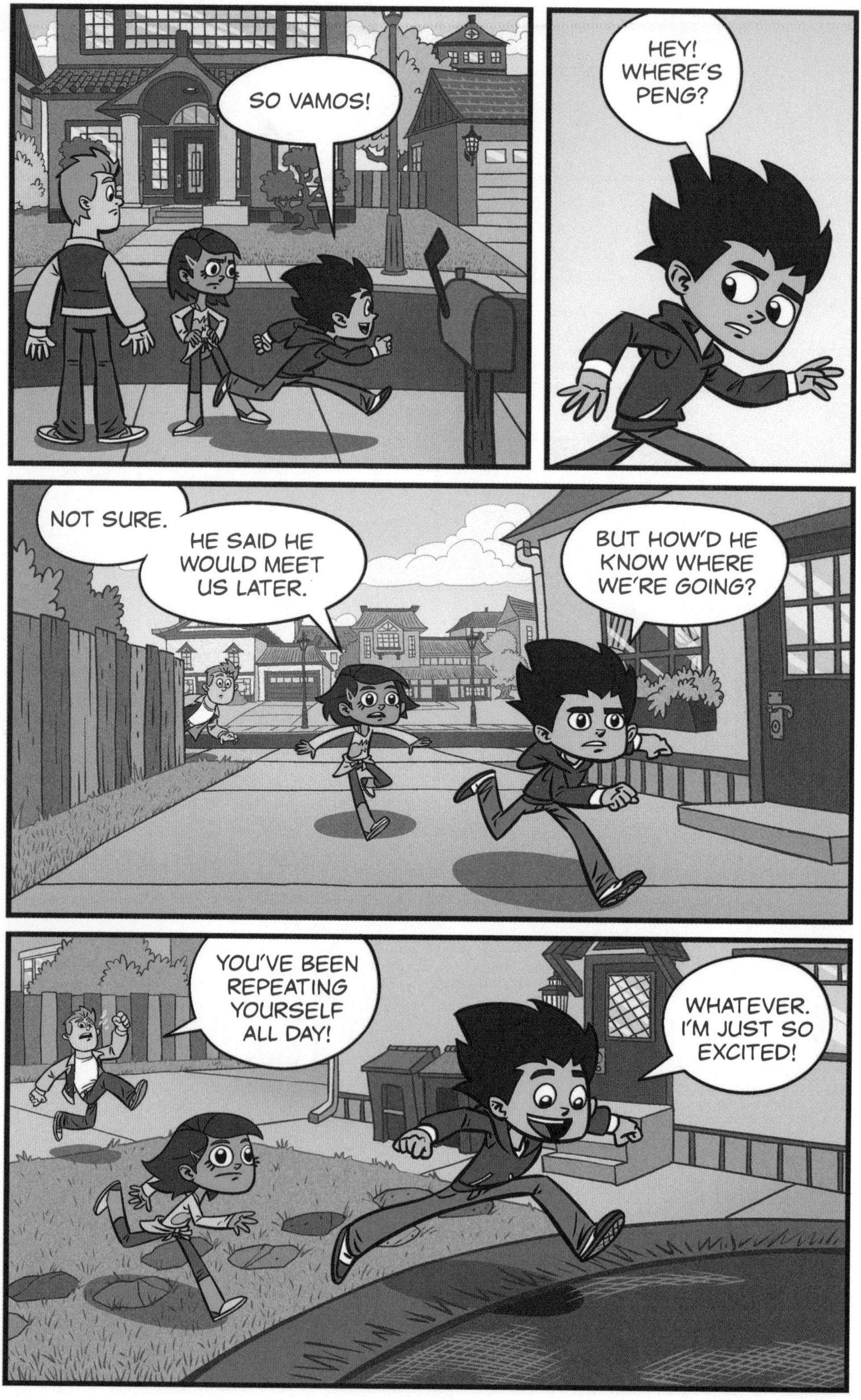
SO VAMOS!
HEY! WHERE'S PENG?
NOT SURE.
HE SAID HE WOULD MEET US LATER.
BUT HOW'D HE KNOW WHERE WE'RE GOING?
YOU'VE BEEN REPEATING YOURSELF ALL DAY!
WHATEVER. I'M JUST SO EXCITED!

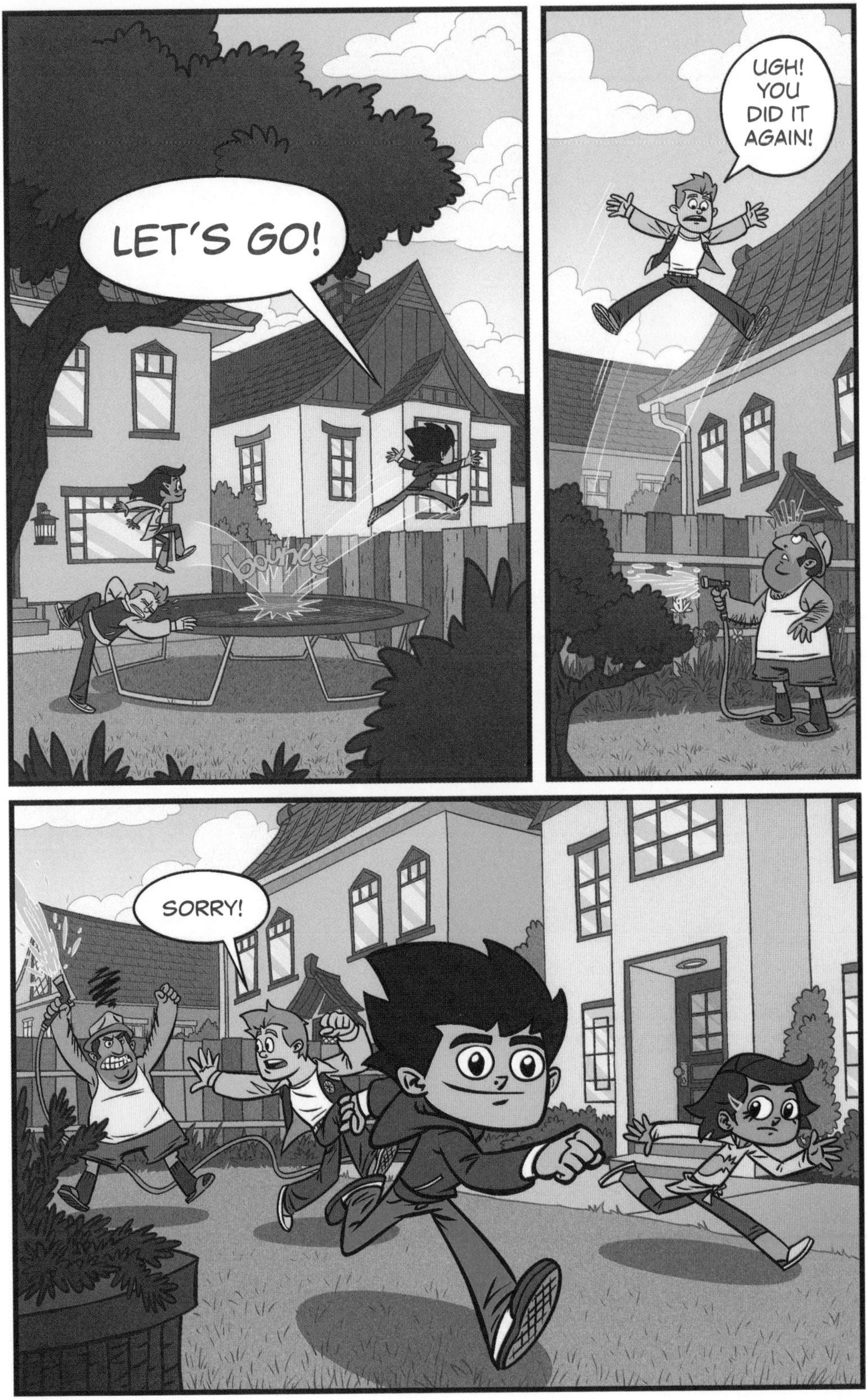
LET'S GO!
bounce
UGH! YOU DID IT AGAIN!
SORRY!

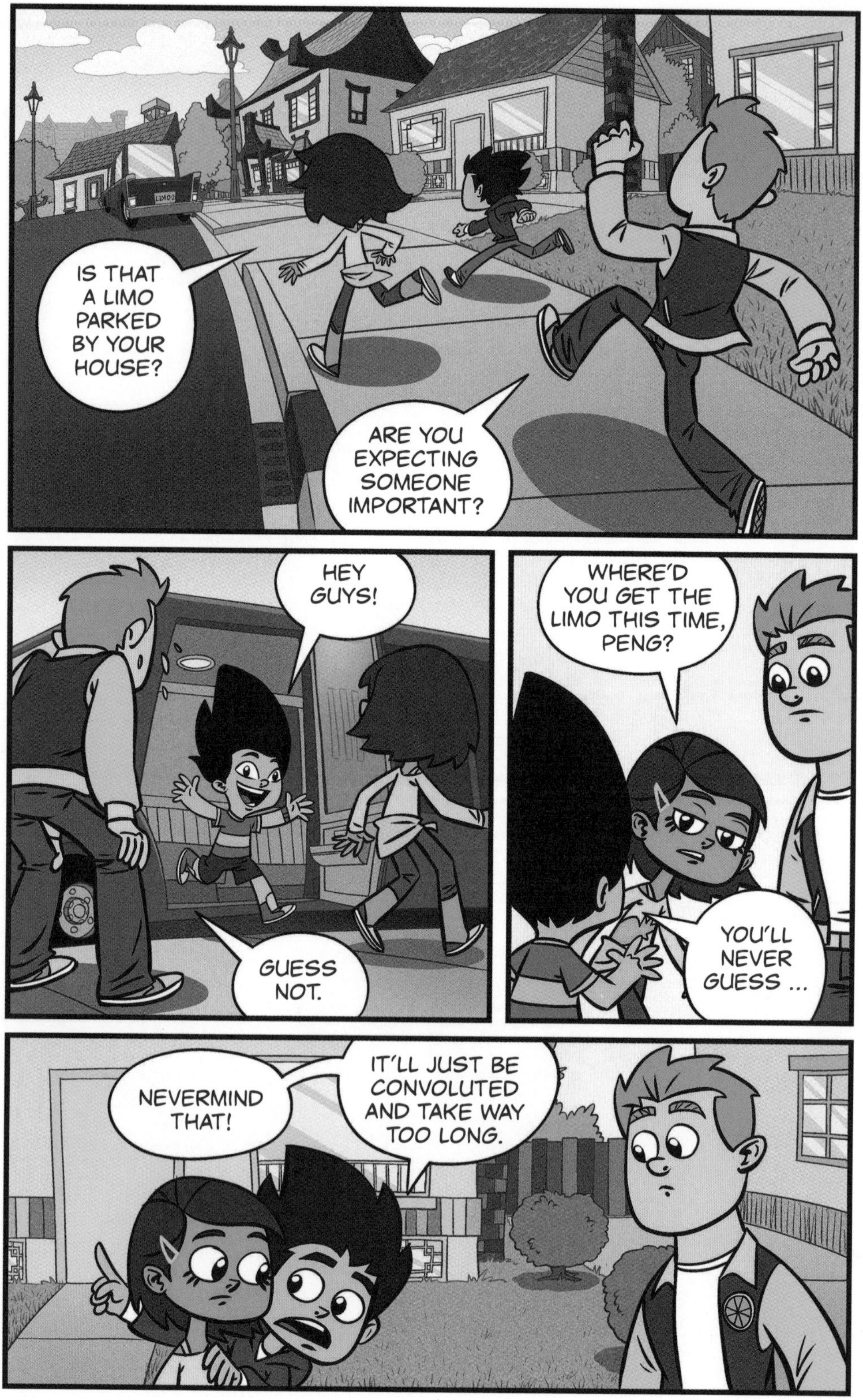
IS THAT A LIMO PARKED BY YOUR HOUSE?
ARE YOU EXPECTING SOMEONE IMPORTANT?
HEY GUYS!
GUESS NOT.
WHERE'D YOU GET THE LIMO THIS TIME, PENG?
YOU'LL NEVER GUESS ...
NEVERMIND THAT!
IT'LL JUST BE CONVOLUTED AND TAKE WAY TOO LONG.

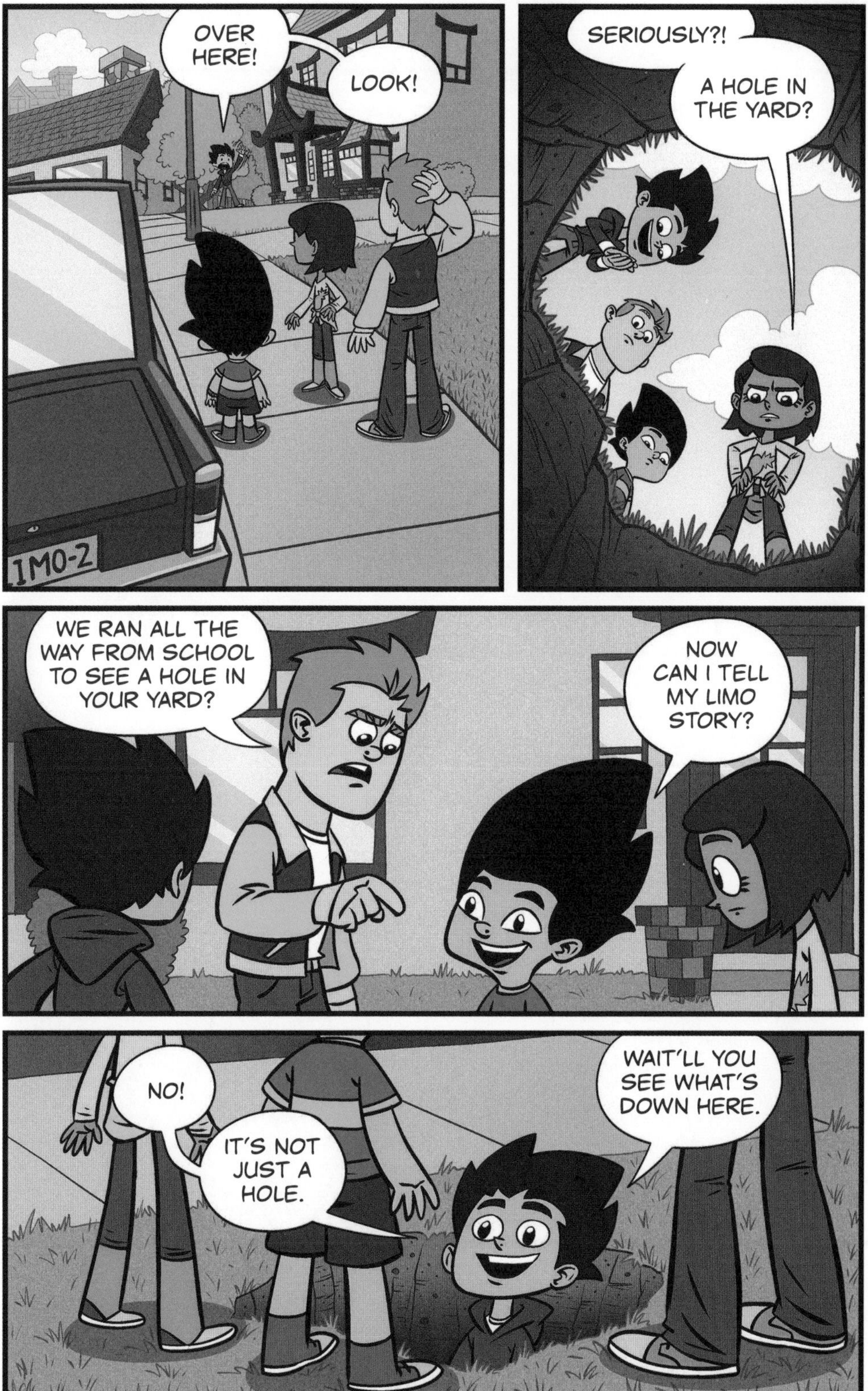
OVER HERE!
LOOK!
IMO-2
SERIOUSLY?!
A HOLE IN THE YARD?
WE RAN ALL THE WAY FROM SCHOOL TO SEE A HOLE IN YOUR YARD?
NOW CAN I TELL MY LIMO STORY?
NO!
IT'S NOT JUST A HOLE.
WAIT'LL YOU SEE WHAT'S DOWN HERE.

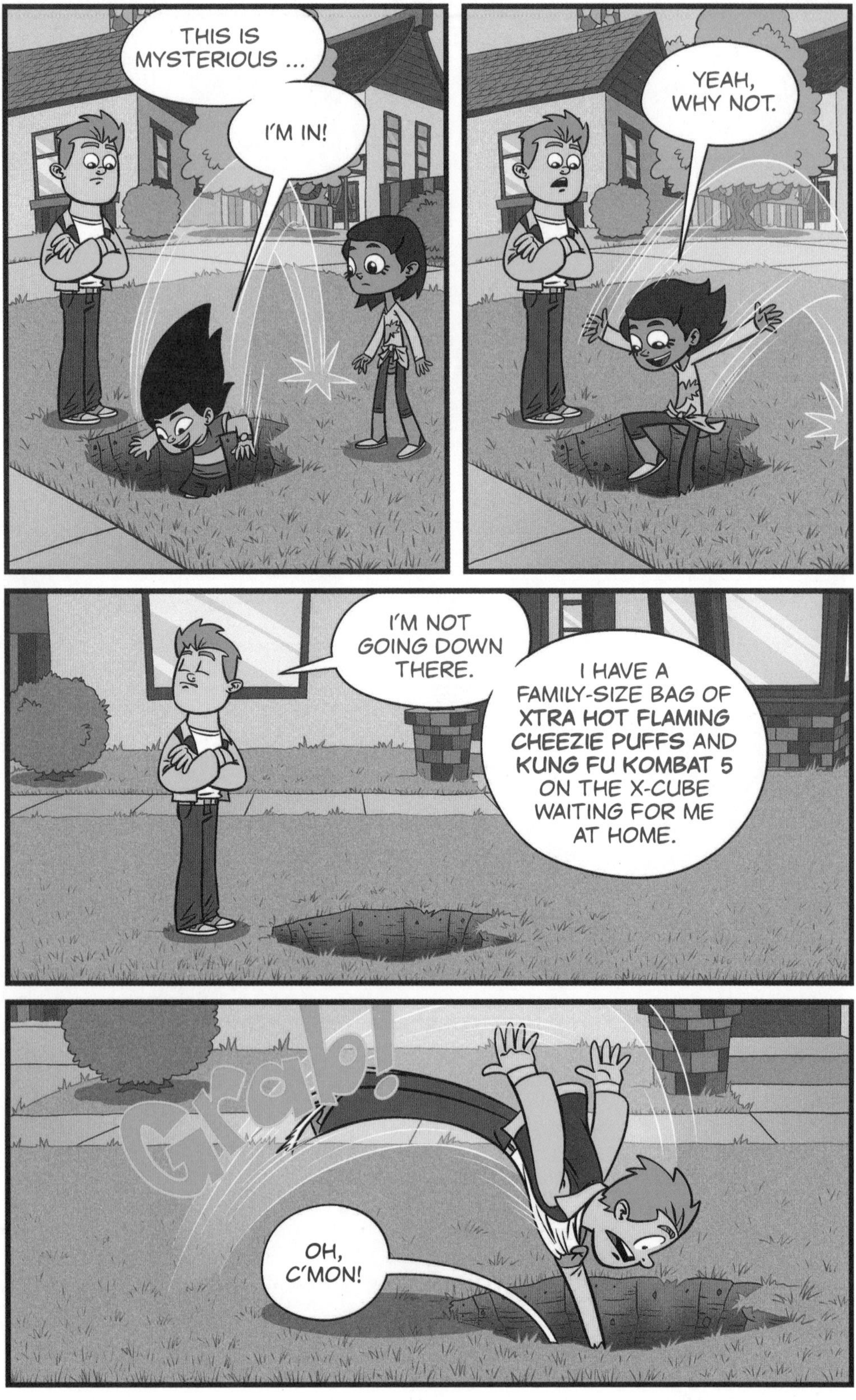
THIS IS MYSTERIOUS ...
I'M IN!
YEAH, WHY NOT.
I'M NOT GOING DOWN THERE.
I HAVE A FAMILY-SIZE BAG OF XTRA HOT FLAMING CHEEZIE PUFFS AND KUNG FU KOMBAT 5 ON THE X-CUBE WAITING FOR ME AT HOME.
Grab!
OH, C'MON!

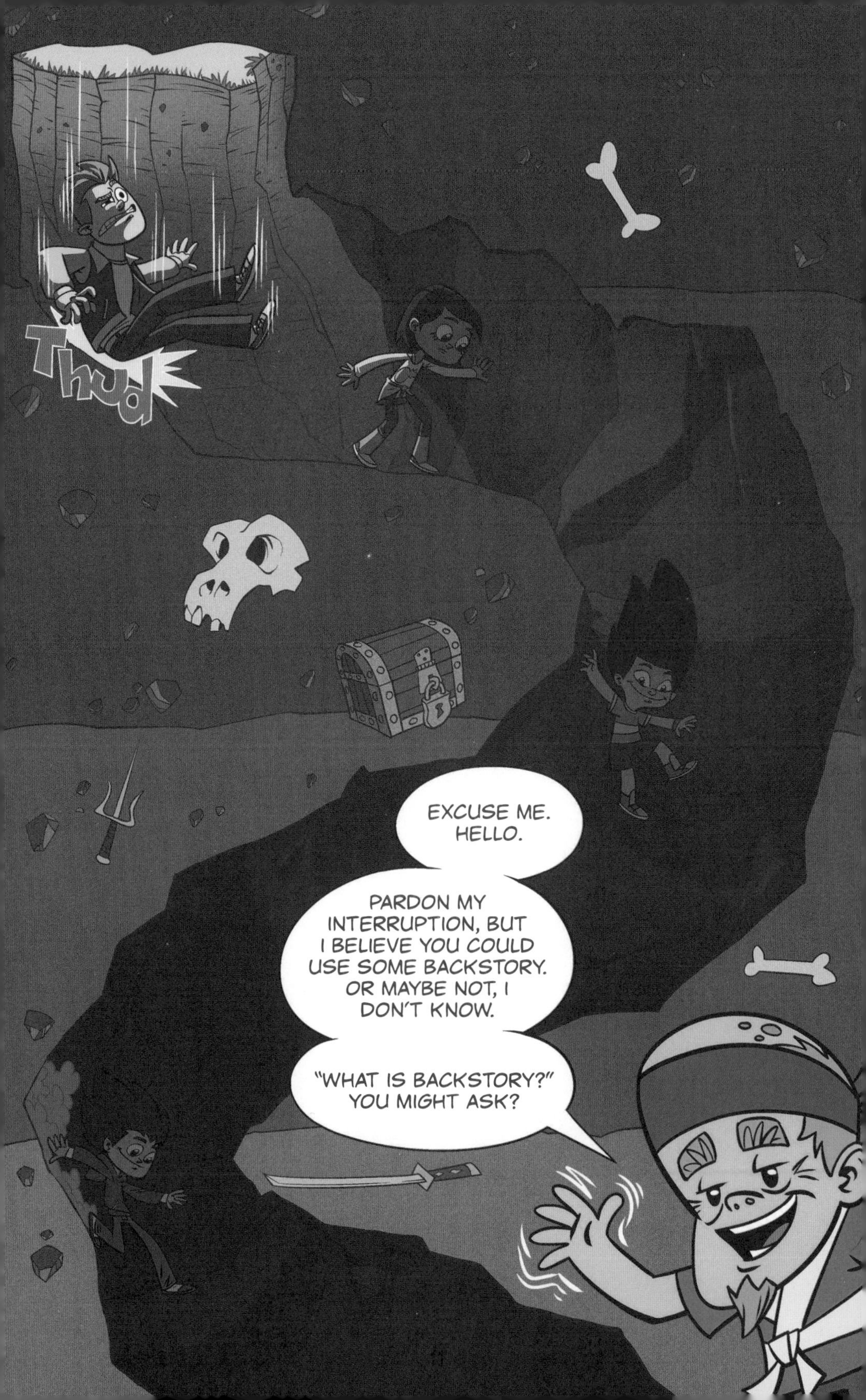
THUD
EXCUSE ME. HELLO.
PARDON MY INTERRUPTION, BUT I BELIEVE YOU COULD USE SOME BACKSTORY. OR MAYBE NOT, I DON'T KNOW.
"WHAT IS BACKSTORY?" YOU MIGHT ASK?

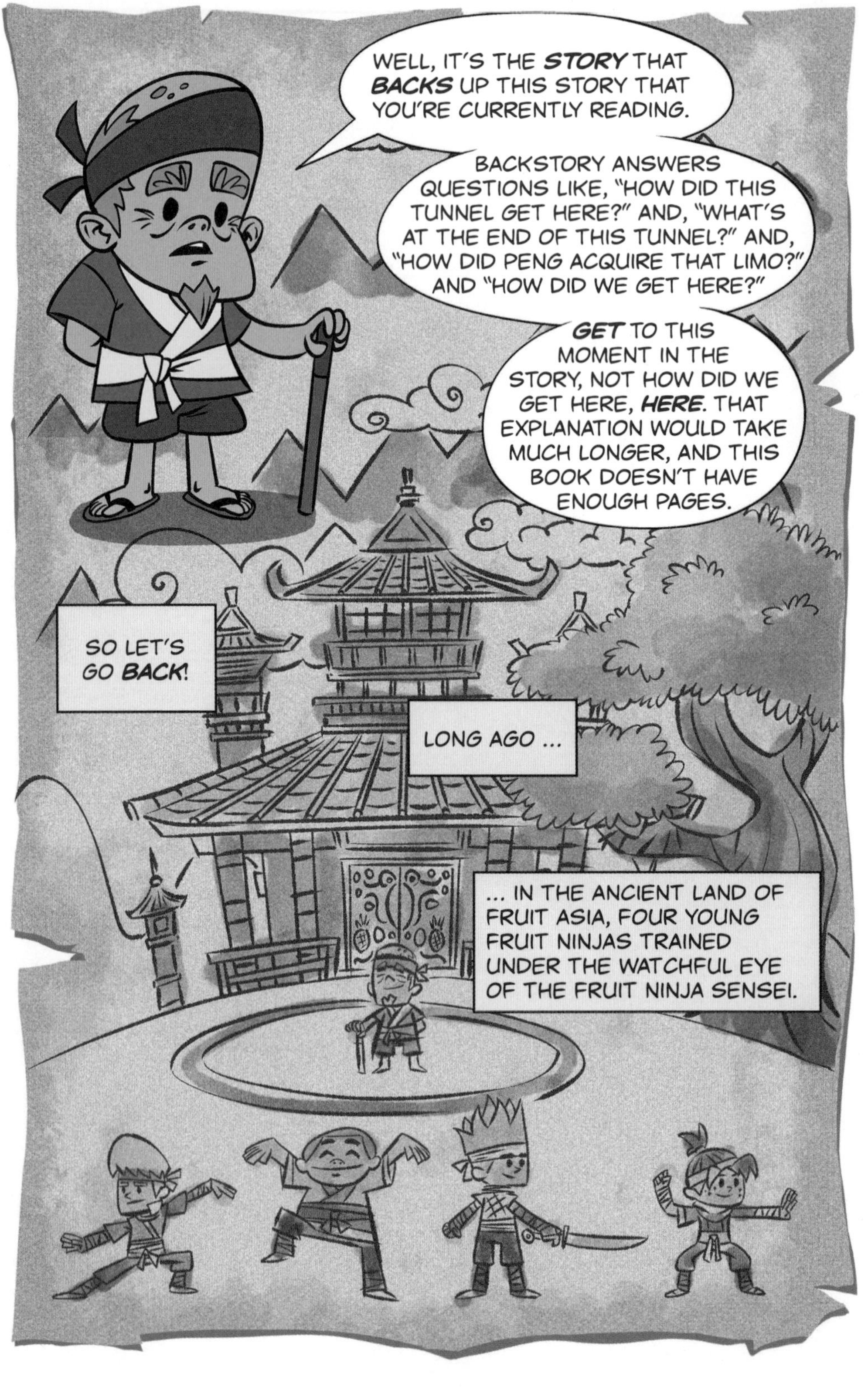

WELL, IT'S THE **STORY** THAT **BACKS** UP THIS STORY THAT YOU'RE CURRENTLY READING.
BACKSTORY ANSWERS QUESTIONS LIKE, "HOW DID THIS TUNNEL GET HERE?" AND, "WHAT'S AT THE END OF THIS TUNNEL?" AND, "HOW DID PENG ACQUIRE THAT LIMO?" AND "HOW DID WE GET HERE?"
GET TO THIS MOMENT IN THE STORY, NOT HOW DID WE GET HERE, **HERE**. THAT EXPLANATION WOULD TAKE MUCH LONGER, AND THIS BOOK DOESN'T HAVE ENOUGH PAGES.
SO LET'S GO **BACK**!
LONG AGO ...
... IN THE ANCIENT LAND OF FRUIT ASIA, FOUR YOUNG FRUIT NINJAS TRAINED UNDER THE WATCHFUL EYE OF THE FRUIT NINJA SENSEI.

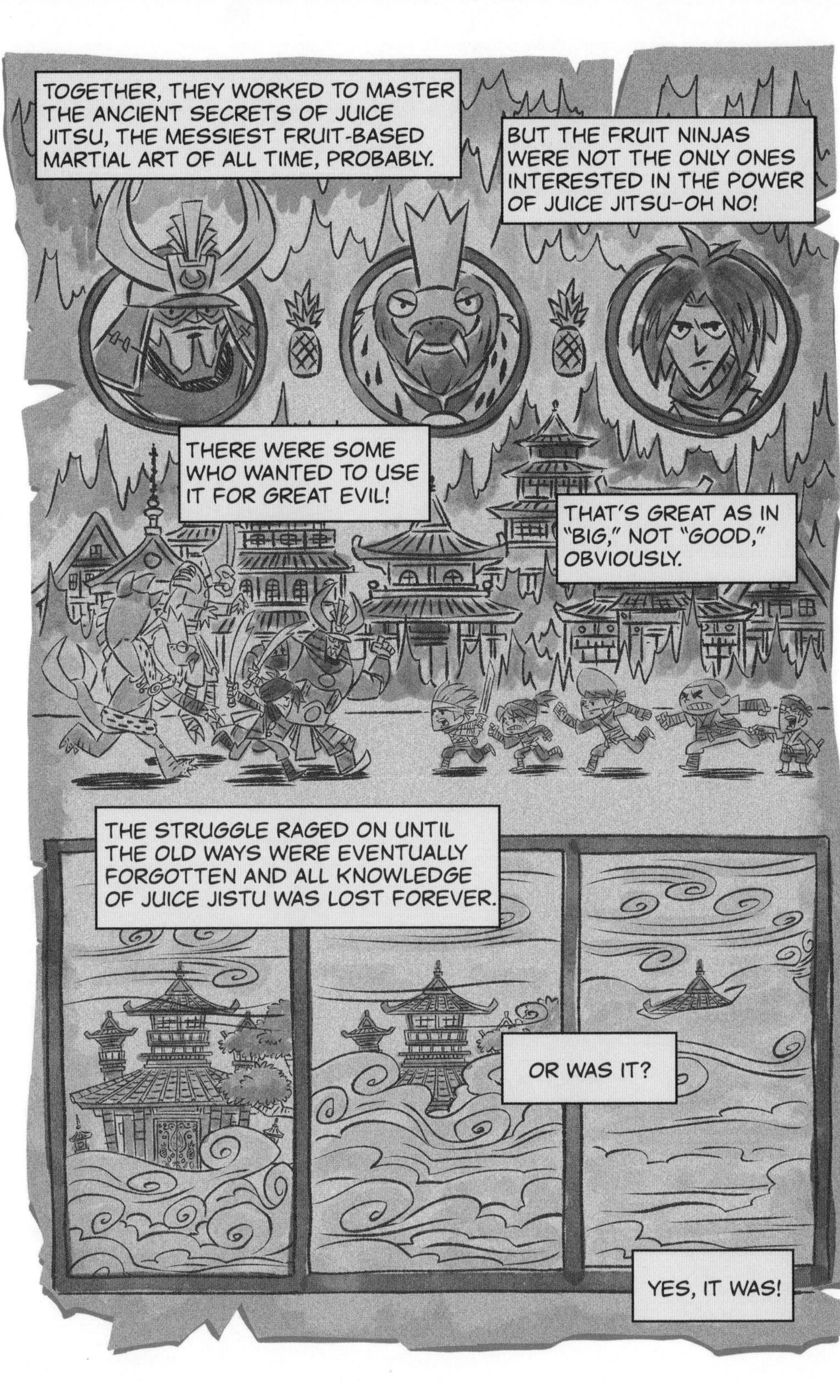
TOGETHER, THEY WORKED TO MASTER THE ANCIENT SECRETS OF JUICE JITSU, THE MESSIEST FRUIT-BASED MARTIAL ART OF ALL TIME, PROBABLY.
BUT THE FRUIT NINJAS WERE NOT THE ONLY ONES INTERESTED IN THE POWER OF JUICE JITSU–OH NO!
THERE WERE SOME WHO WANTED TO USE IT FOR GREAT EVIL!
THAT'S GREAT AS IN "BIG," NOT "GOOD," OBVIOUSLY.
THE STRUGGLE RAGED ON UNTIL THE OLD WAYS WERE EVENTUALLY FORGOTTEN AND ALL KNOWLEDGE OF JUICE JISTU WAS LOST FOREVER.
OR WAS IT?
YES, IT WAS!

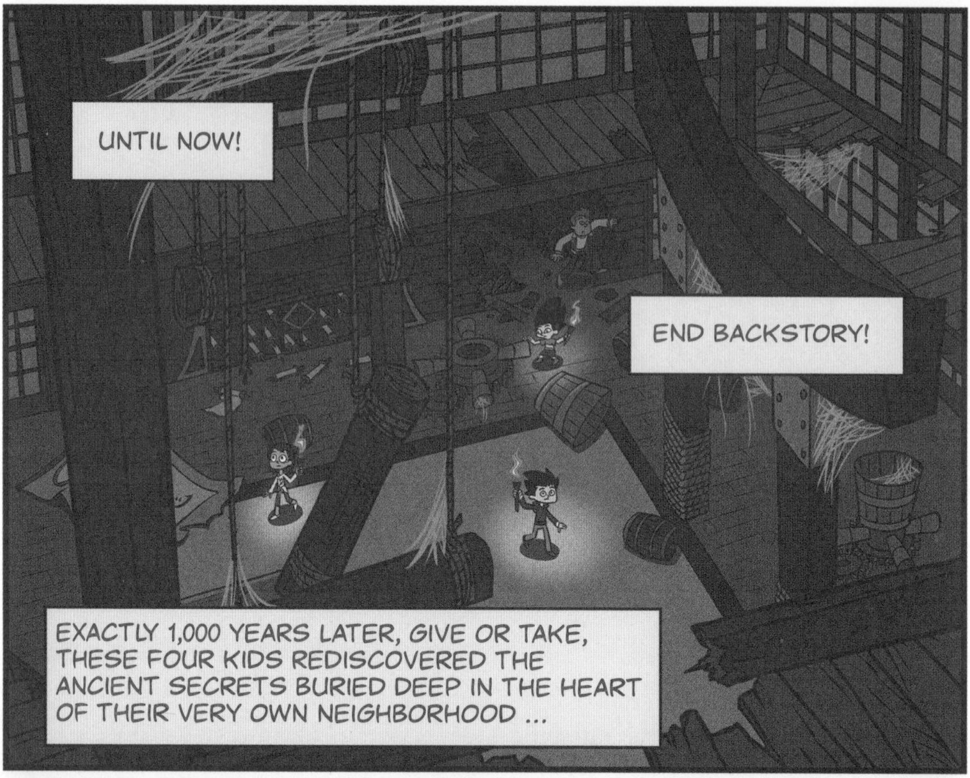
UNTIL NOW!
END BACKSTORY!
EXACTLY 1,000 YEARS LATER, GIVE OR TAKE, THESE FOUR KIDS REDISCOVERED THE ANCIENT SECRETS BURIED DEEP IN THE HEART OF THEIR VERY OWN NEIGHBORHOOD ...

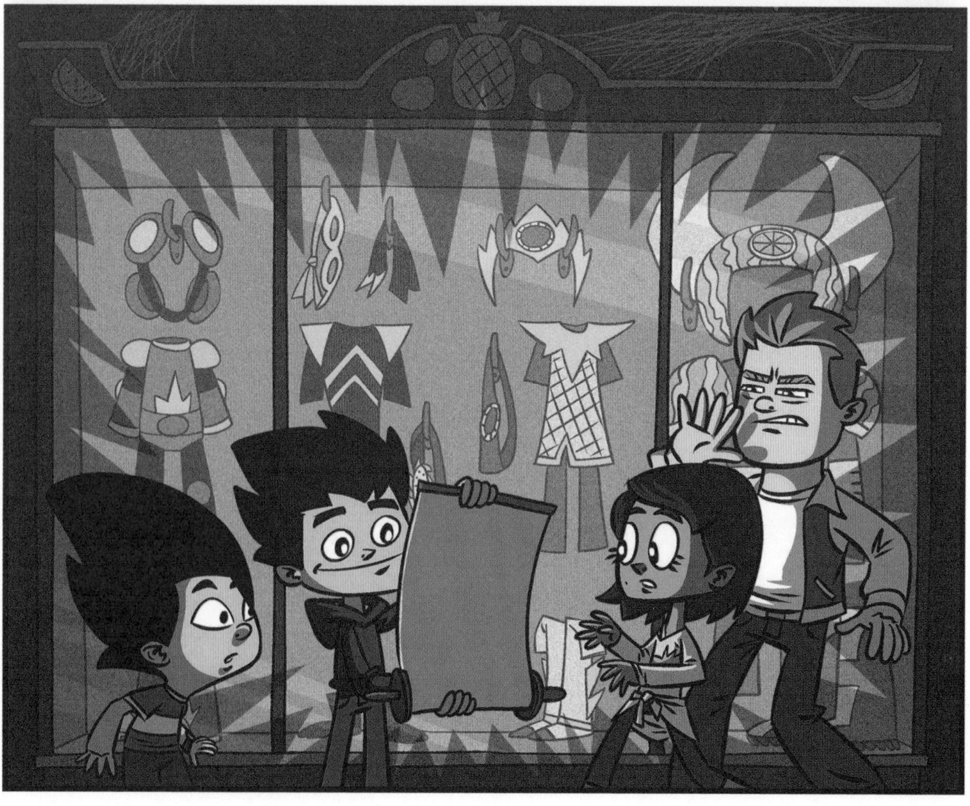

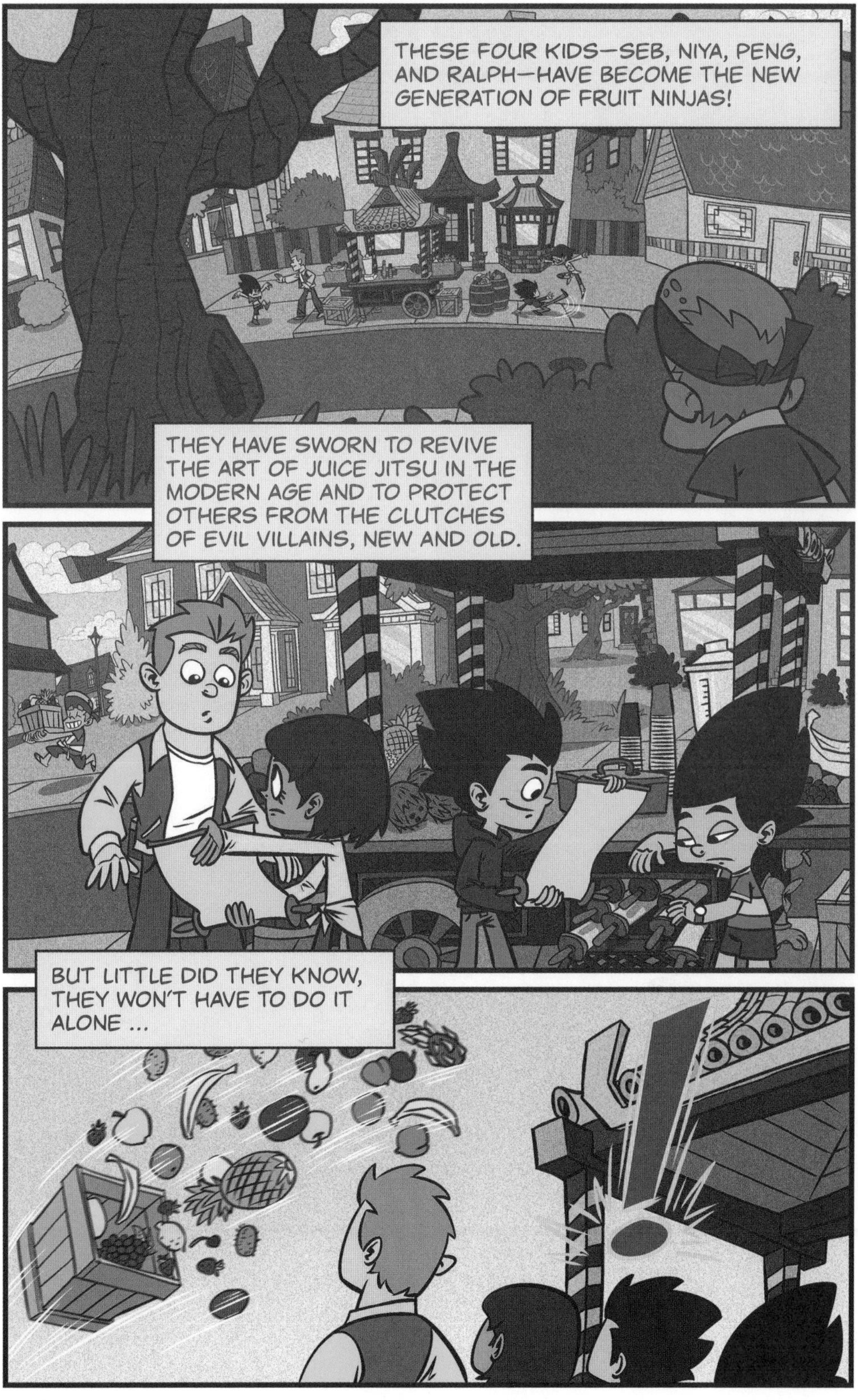
THESE FOUR KIDS—SEB, NIYA, PENG, AND RALPH—HAVE BECOME THE NEW GENERATION OF FRUIT NINJAS!
THEY HAVE SWORN TO REVIVE THE ART OF JUICE JITSU IN THE MODERN AGE AND TO PROTECT OTHERS FROM THE CLUTCHES OF EVIL VILLAINS, NEW AND OLD.
BUT LITTLE DID THEY KNOW, THEY WON'T HAVE TO DO IT ALONE ...

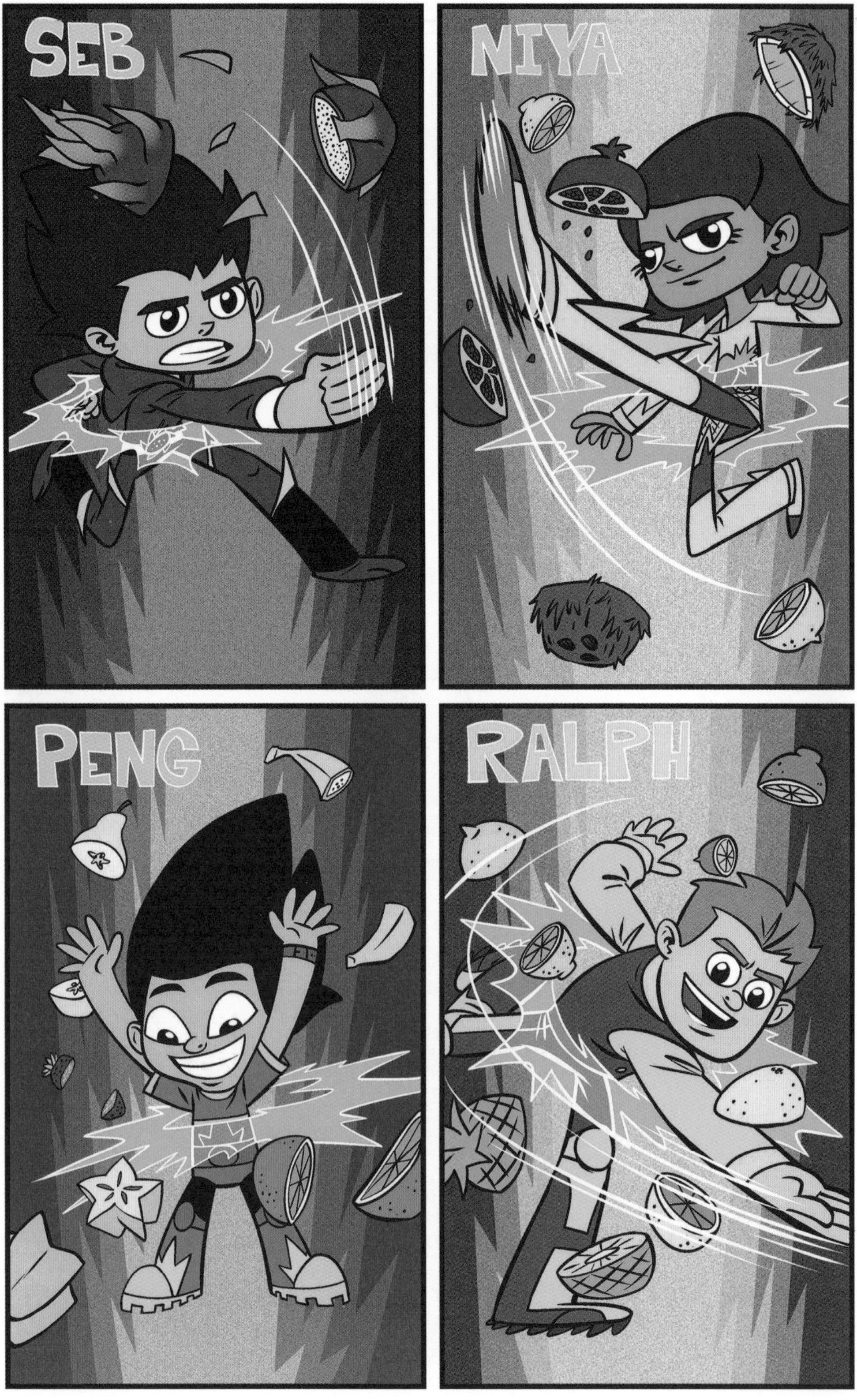
SEB
NIYA
PENG
RALPH

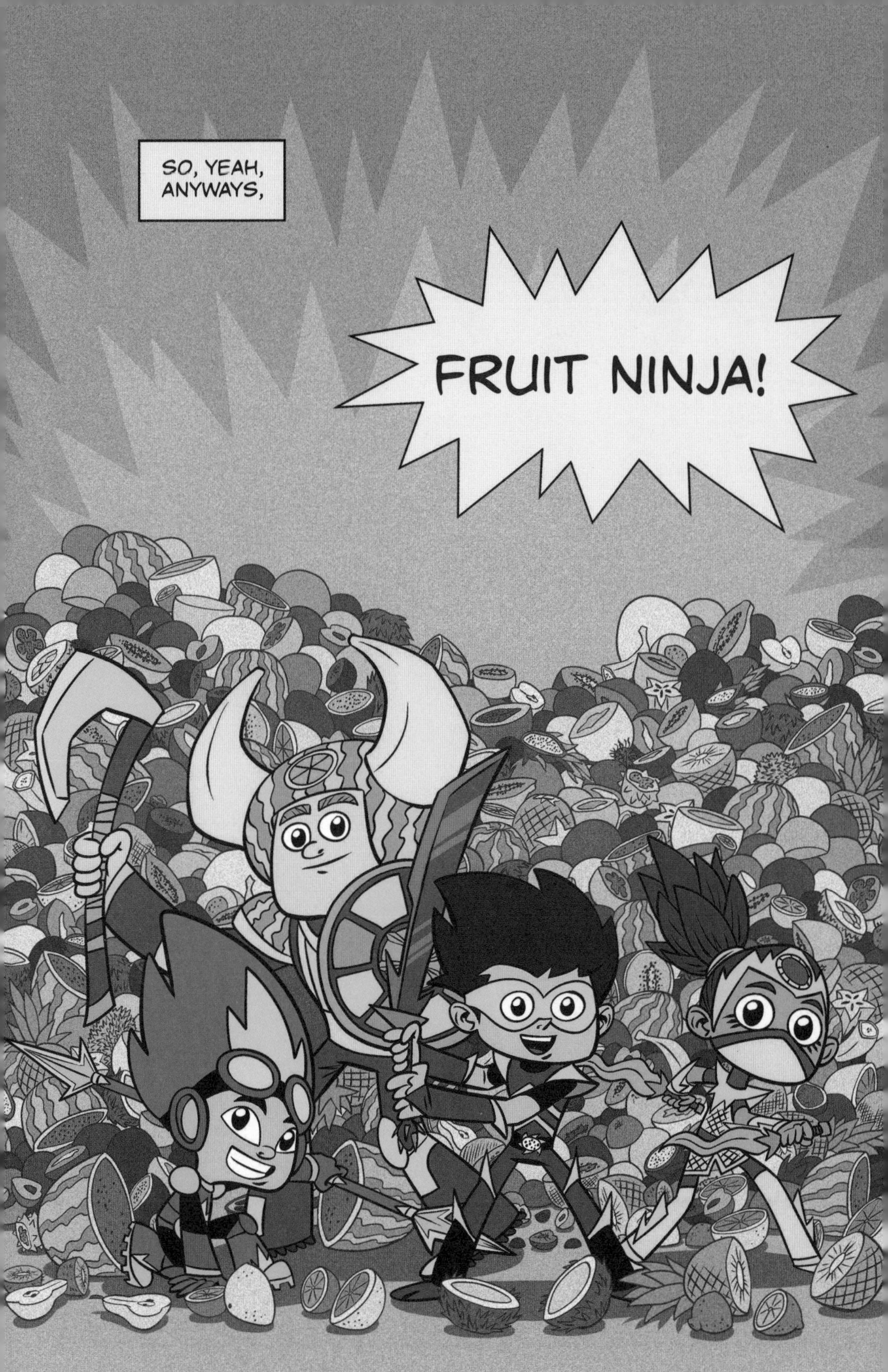
SO, YEAH, ANYWAYS,
FRUIT NINJA!

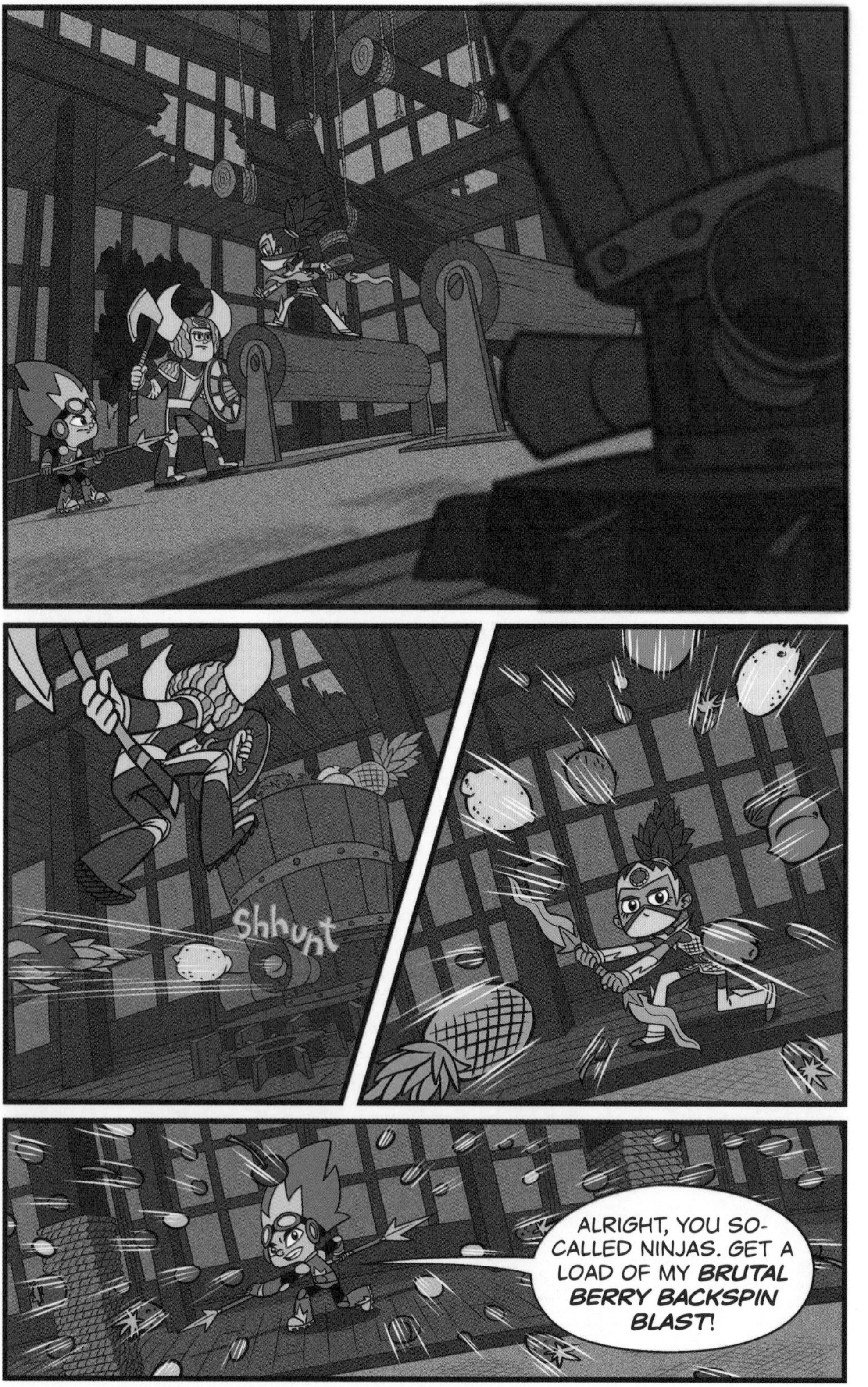
Shhunt
ALRIGHT, YOU SO-CALLED NINJAS. GET A LOAD OF MY ***BRUTAL BERRY BACKSPIN BLAST***!

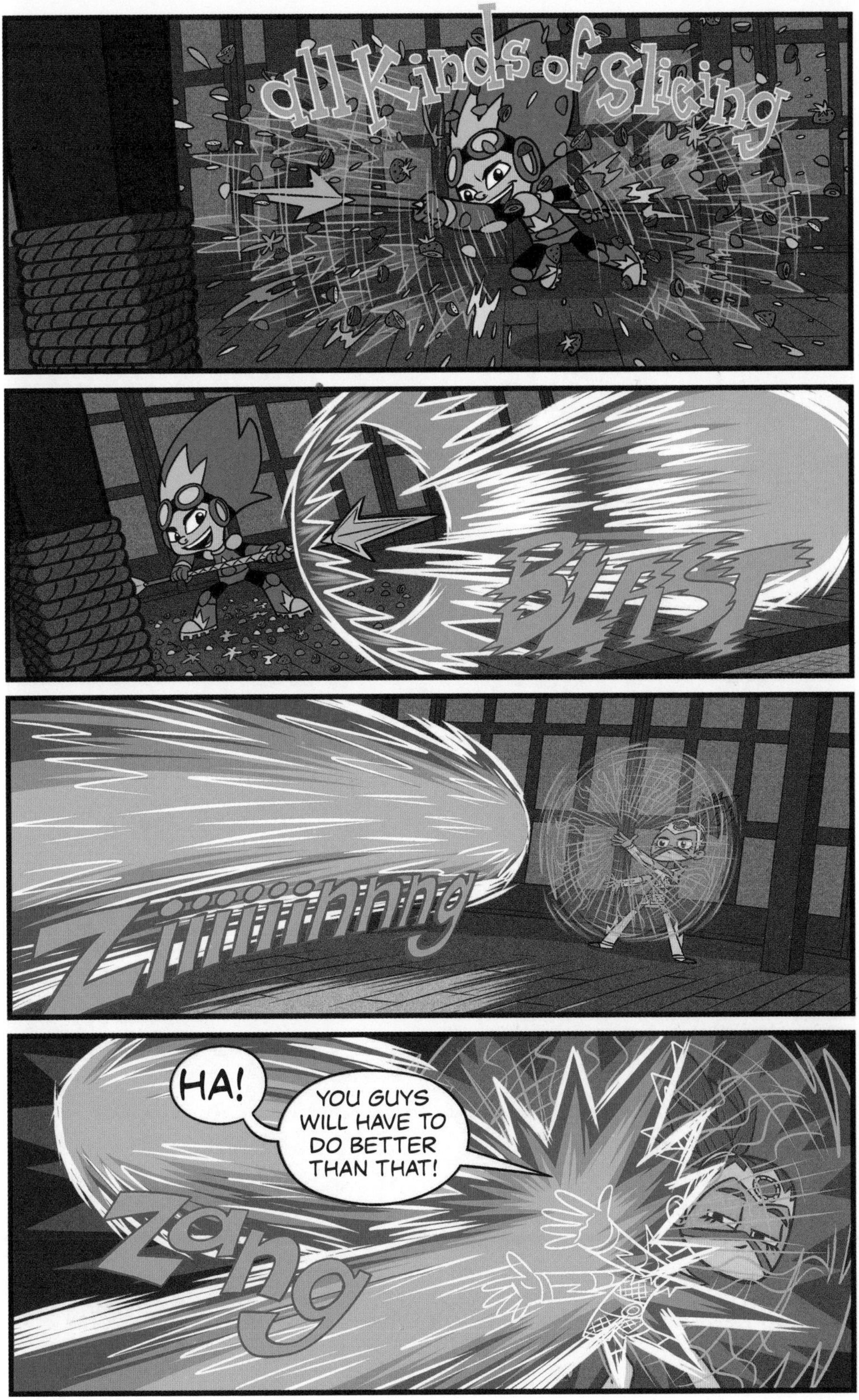
all Kinds of Slicing
BLAST
Ziiiiiinnng
HA!
YOU GUYS WILL HAVE TO DO BETTER THAN THAT!
Zang

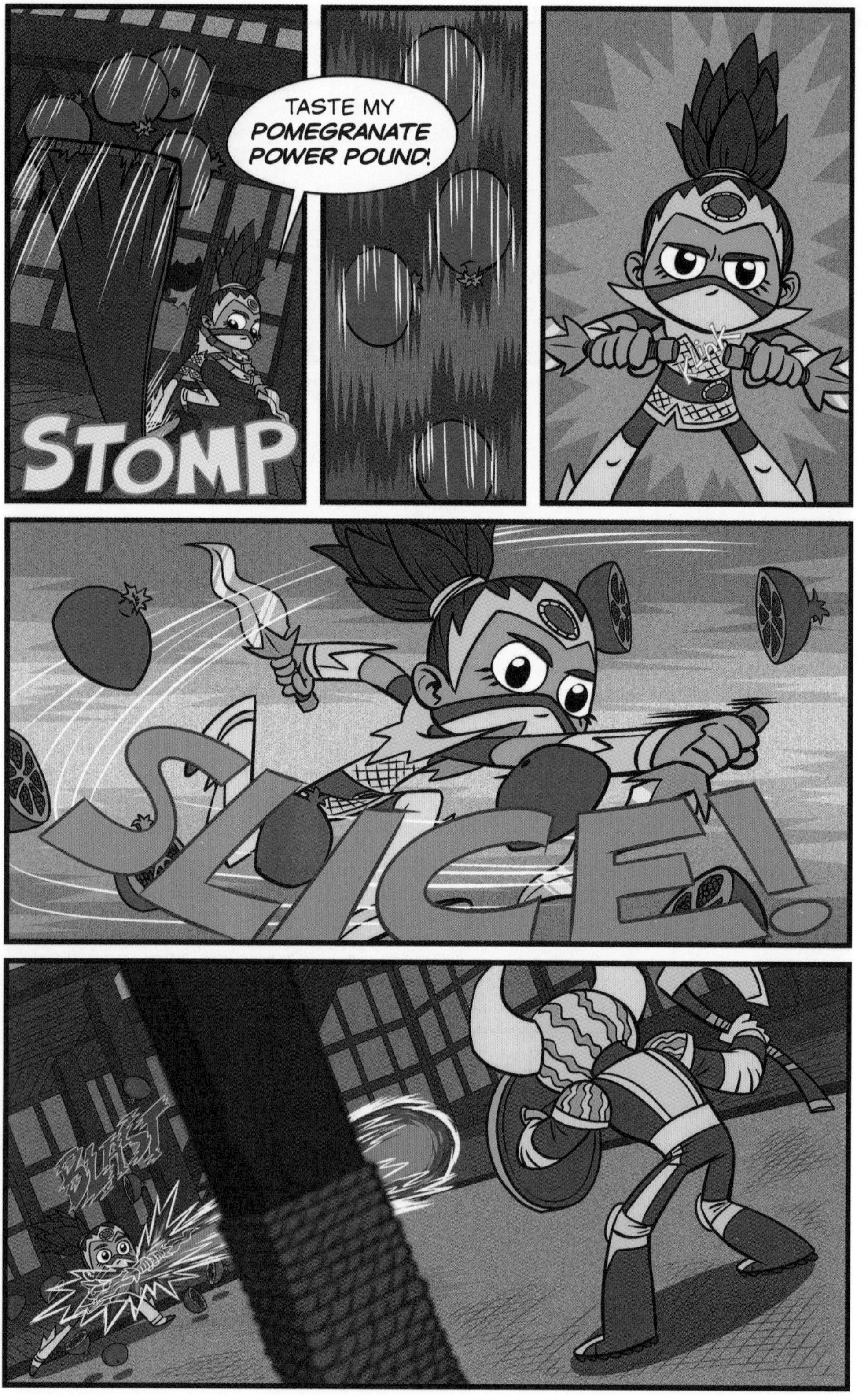
TASTE MY *POMEGRANATE POWER POUND!*
STOMP
Klink
SLICE!
BLAST

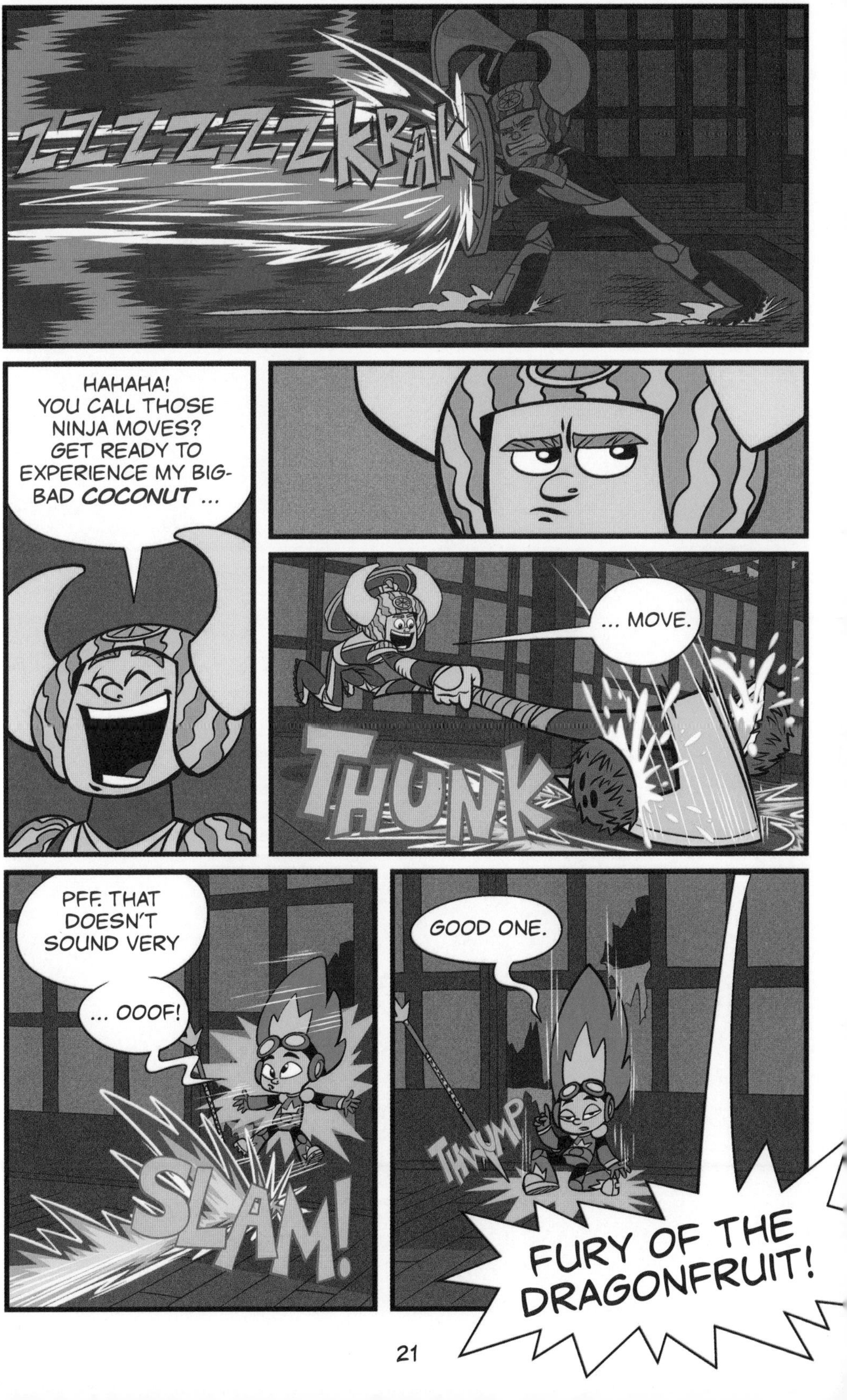
ZZZZZZZKRAK
HAHAHA! YOU CALL THOSE NINJA MOVES? GET READY TO EXPERIENCE MY BIG-BAD COCONUT ...
... MOVE.
THUNK
PFF. THAT DOESN'T SOUND VERY
... OOOF!
SLAM!
GOOD ONE.
THWUMP
FURY OF THE DRAGONFRUIT!

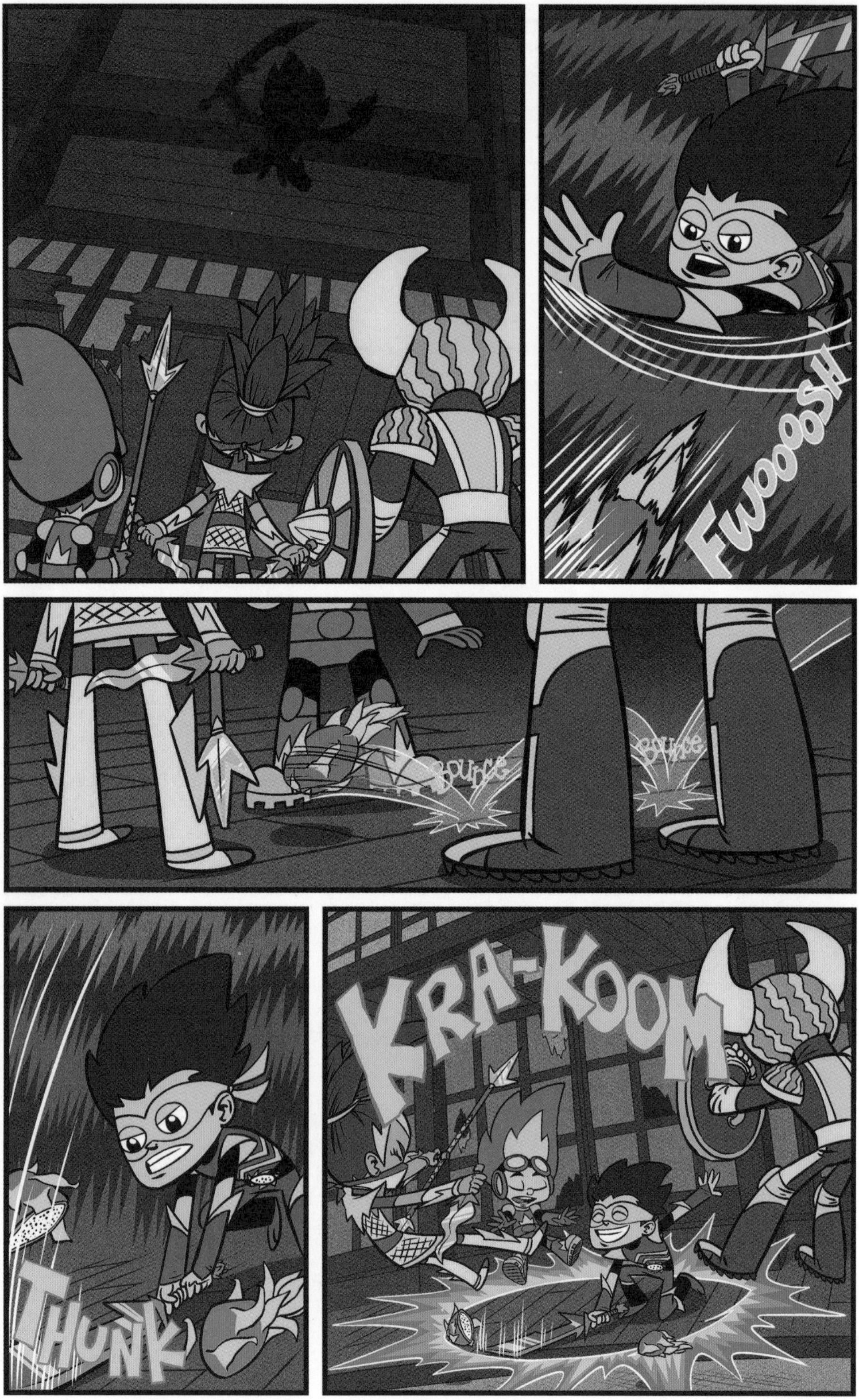
FWOOOOSH
BOUNCE
BOUNCE
THUNK
KRA-KOOM

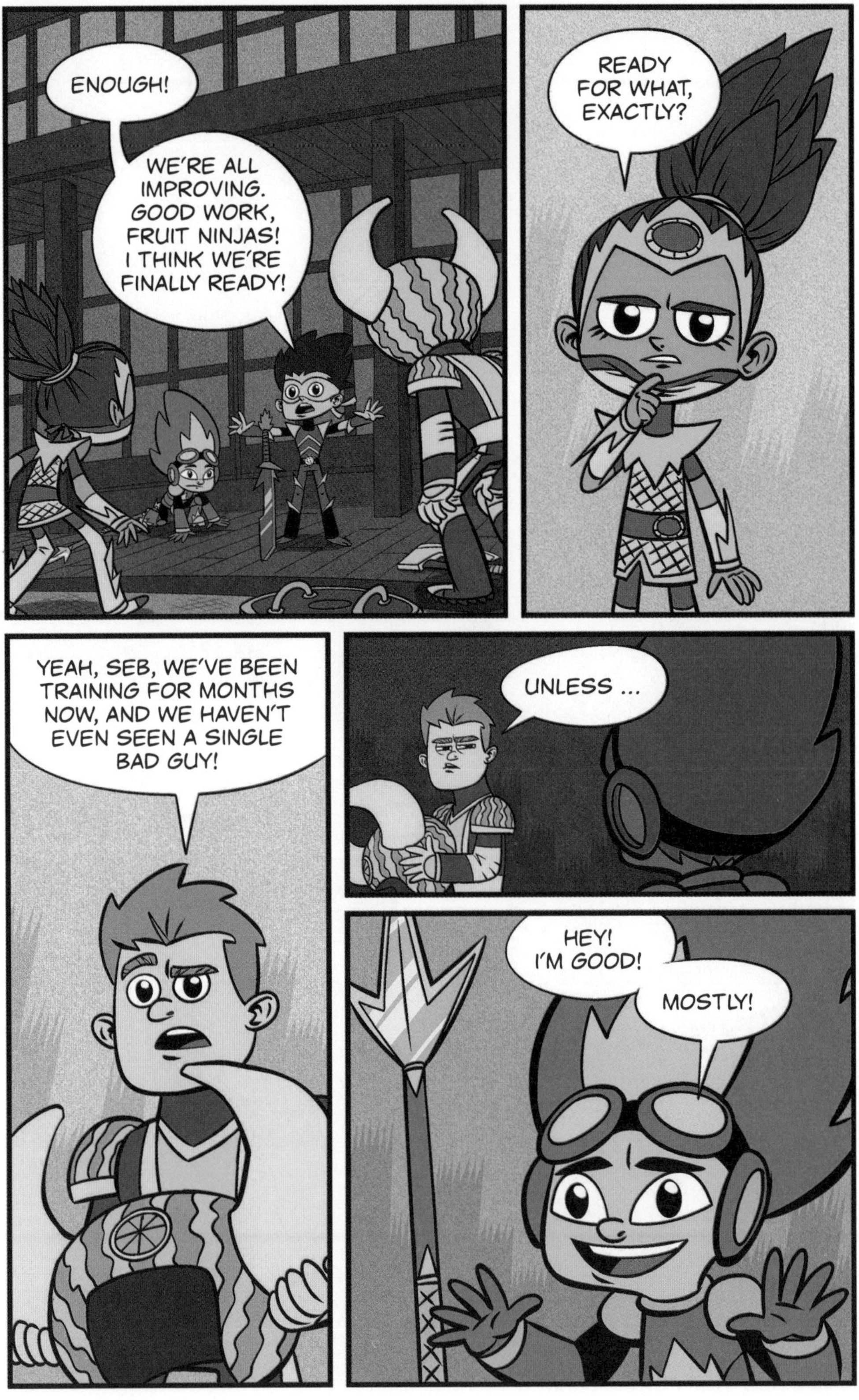
ENOUGH!
WE'RE ALL IMPROVING. GOOD WORK, FRUIT NINJAS! I THINK WE'RE FINALLY READY!
READY FOR WHAT, EXACTLY?
YEAH, SEB, WE'VE BEEN TRAINING FOR MONTHS NOW, AND WE HAVEN'T EVEN SEEN A SINGLE BAD GUY!
UNLESS ...
HEY! I'M GOOD!
MOSTLY!

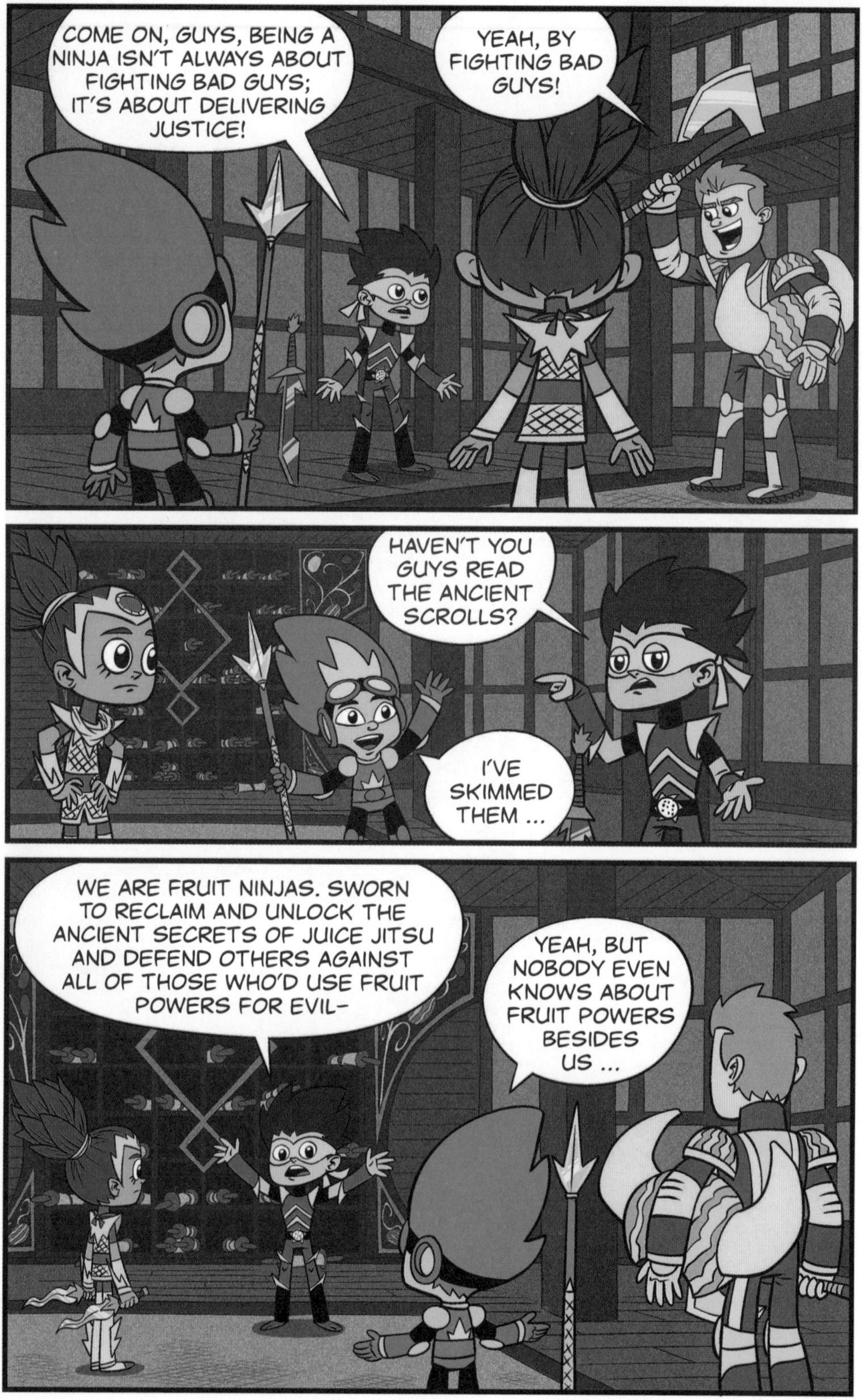
COME ON, GUYS, BEING A NINJA ISN'T ALWAYS ABOUT FIGHTING BAD GUYS; IT'S ABOUT DELIVERING JUSTICE!
YEAH, BY FIGHTING BAD GUYS!
HAVEN'T YOU GUYS READ THE ANCIENT SCROLLS?
I'VE SKIMMED THEM ...
WE ARE FRUIT NINJAS. SWORN TO RECLAIM AND UNLOCK THE ANCIENT SECRETS OF JUICE JITSU AND DEFEND OTHERS AGAINST ALL OF THOSE WHO'D USE FRUIT POWERS FOR EVIL-
YEAH, BUT NOBODY EVEN KNOWS ABOUT FRUIT POWERS BESIDES US ...

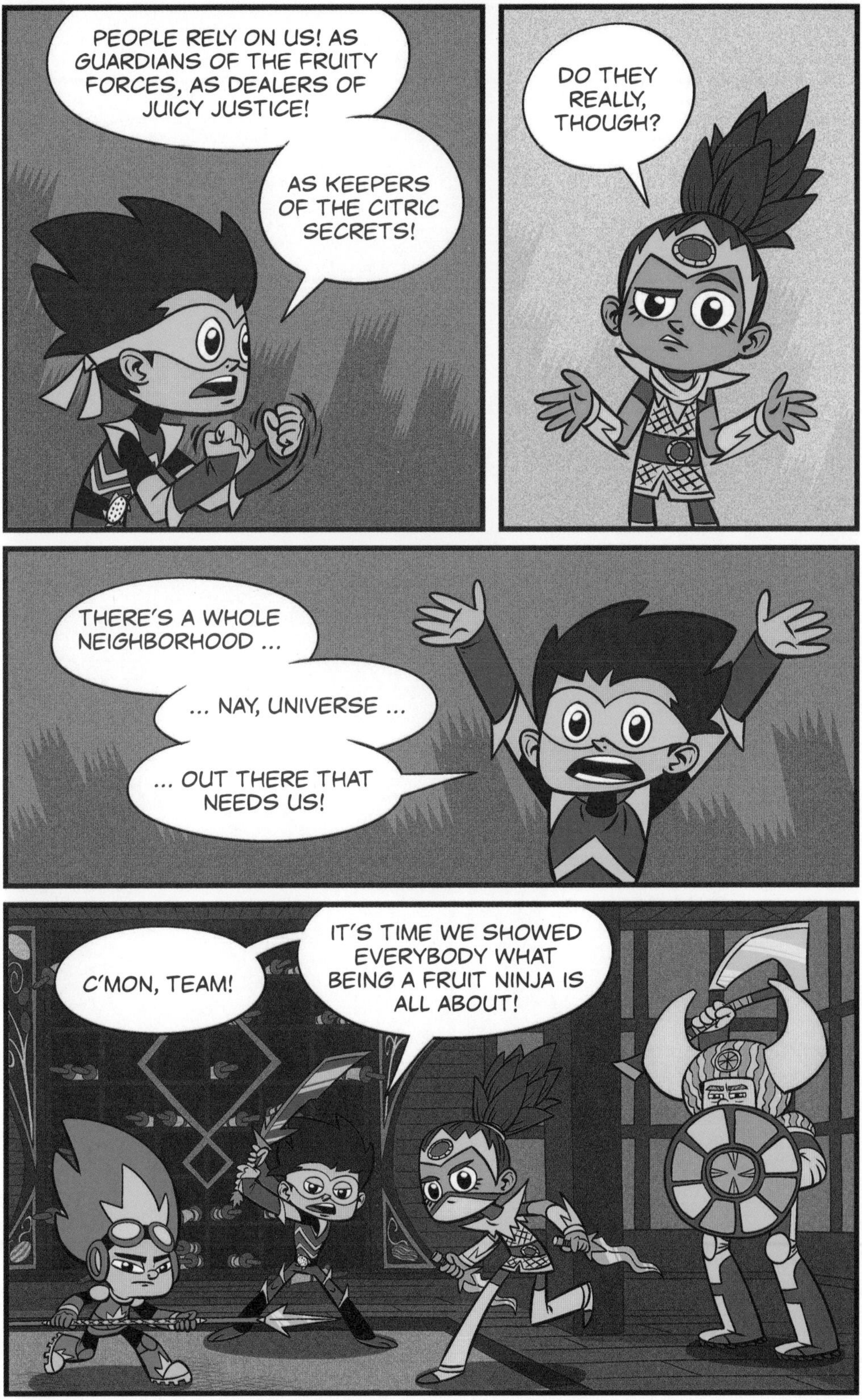
PEOPLE RELY ON US! AS GUARDIANS OF THE FRUITY FORCES, AS DEALERS OF JUICY JUSTICE!
AS KEEPERS OF THE CITRIC SECRETS!
DO THEY REALLY, THOUGH?
THERE'S A WHOLE NEIGHBORHOOD ...
... NAY, UNIVERSE ...
... OUT THERE THAT NEEDS US!
C'MON, TEAM!
IT'S TIME WE SHOWED EVERYBODY WHAT BEING A FRUIT NINJA IS ALL ABOUT!

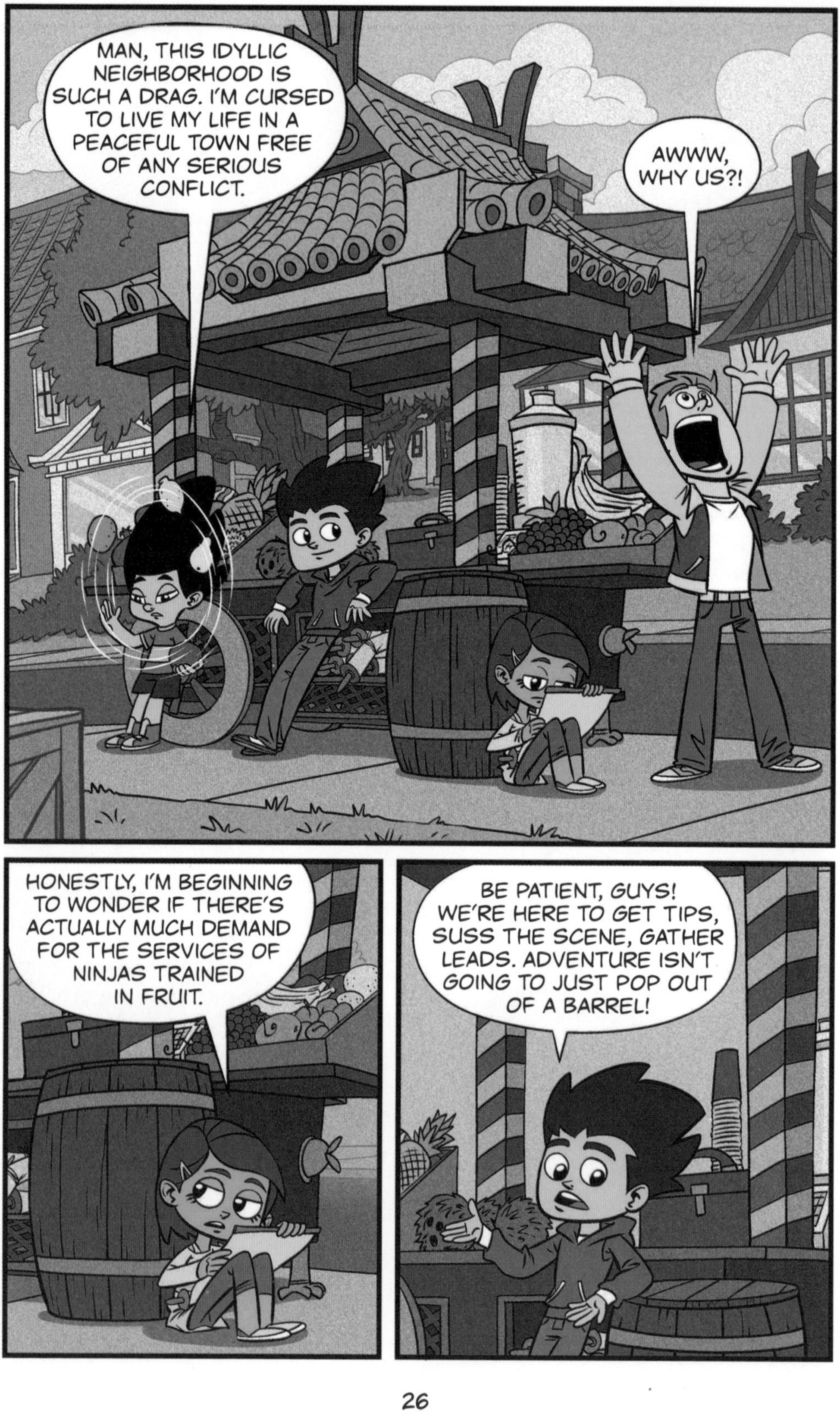
MAN, THIS IDYLLIC NEIGHBORHOOD IS SUCH A DRAG. I'M CURSED TO LIVE MY LIFE IN A PEACEFUL TOWN FREE OF ANY SERIOUS CONFLICT.
AWWW, WHY US?!
HONESTLY, I'M BEGINNING TO WONDER IF THERE'S ACTUALLY MUCH DEMAND FOR THE SERVICES OF NINJAS TRAINED IN FRUIT.
BE PATIENT, GUYS! WE'RE HERE TO GET TIPS, SUSS THE SCENE, GATHER LEADS. ADVENTURE ISN'T GOING TO JUST POP OUT OF A BARREL!

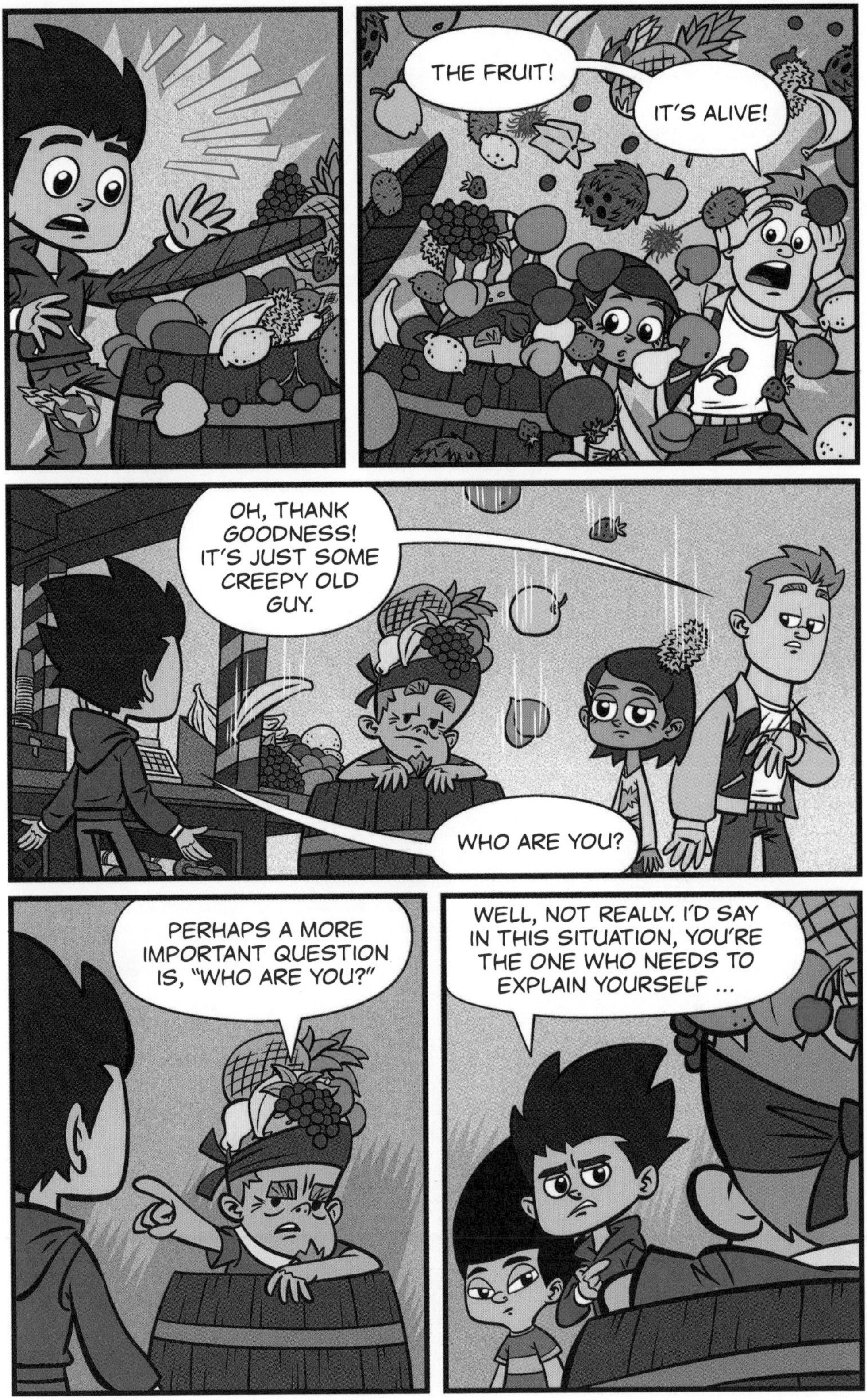
THE FRUIT!
IT'S ALIVE!
OH, THANK GOODNESS! IT'S JUST SOME CREEPY OLD GUY.
WHO ARE YOU?
PERHAPS A MORE IMPORTANT QUESTION IS, "WHO ARE YOU?"
WELL, NOT REALLY. I'D SAY IN THIS SITUATION, YOU'RE THE ONE WHO NEEDS TO EXPLAIN YOURSELF ...

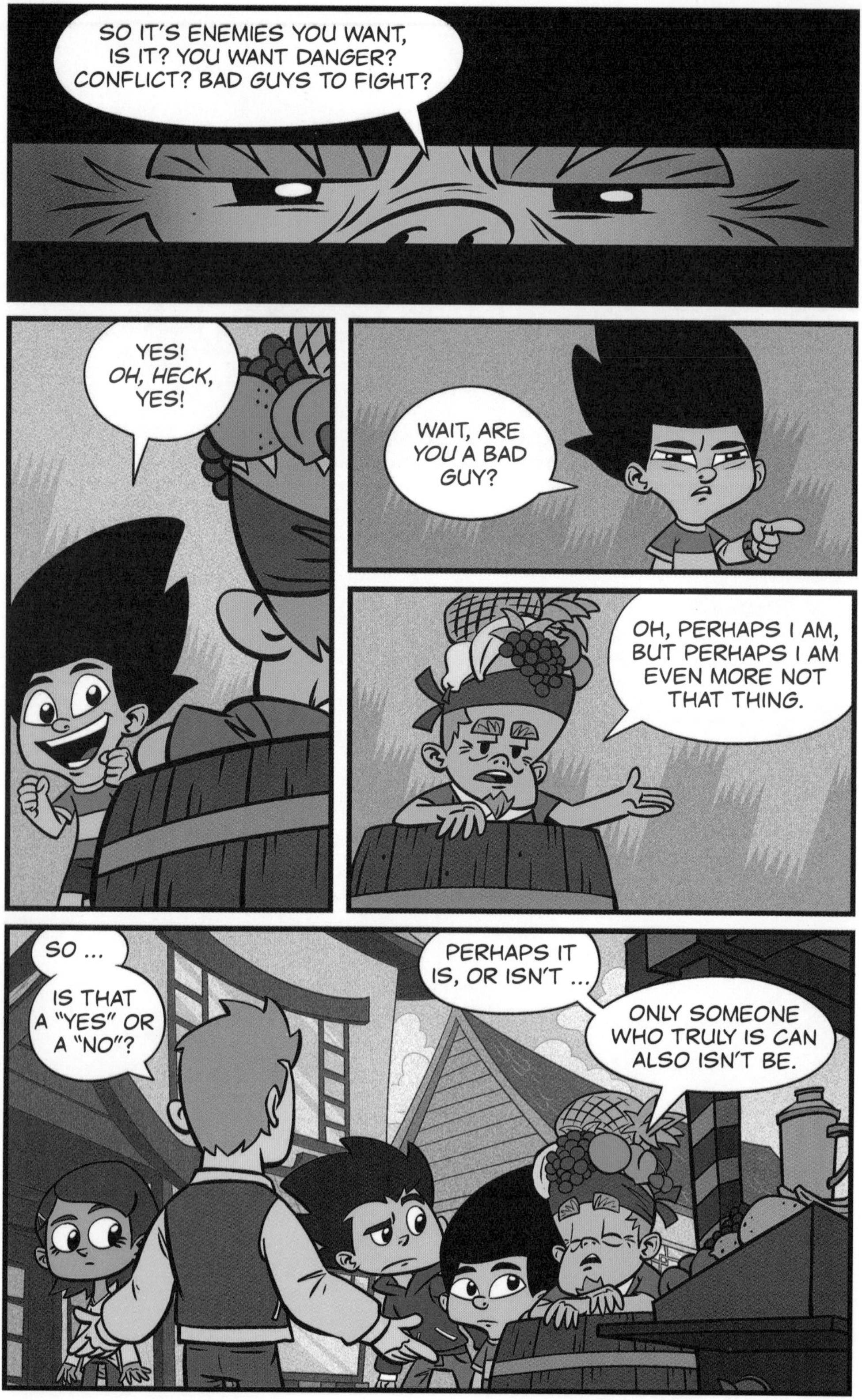
SO IT'S ENEMIES YOU WANT, IS IT? YOU WANT DANGER? CONFLICT? BAD GUYS TO FIGHT?
YES! OH, HECK, YES!
WAIT, ARE YOU A BAD GUY?
OH, PERHAPS I AM, BUT PERHAPS I AM EVEN MORE NOT THAT THING.
SO ...
IS THAT A "YES" OR A "NO"?
PERHAPS IT IS, OR ISN'T ...
ONLY SOMEONE WHO TRULY IS CAN ALSO ISN'T BE.

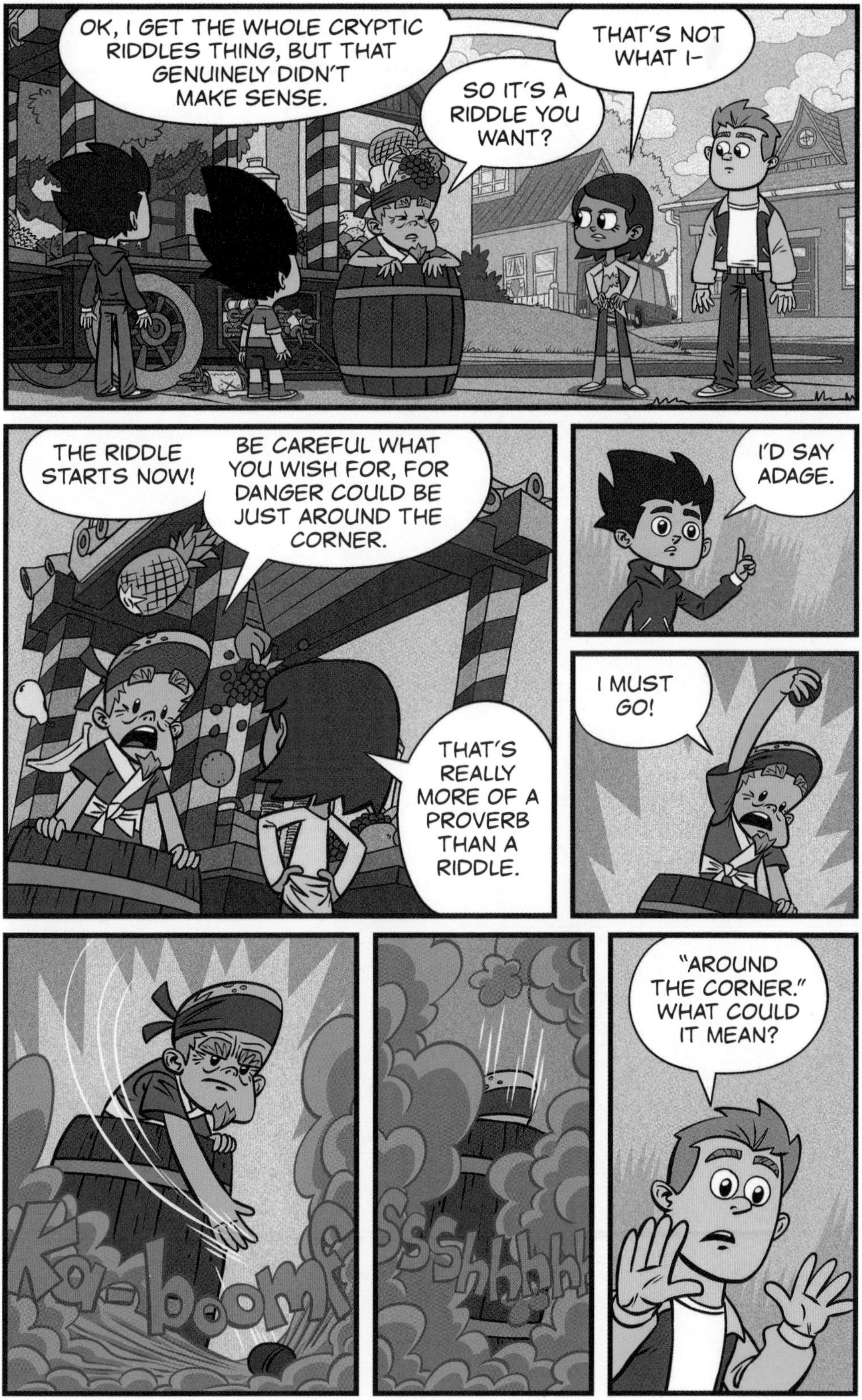

OK, I GET THE WHOLE CRYPTIC RIDDLES THING, BUT THAT GENUINELY DIDN'T MAKE SENSE.
SO IT'S A RIDDLE YOU WANT?
THAT'S NOT WHAT I–
THE RIDDLE STARTS NOW!
BE CAREFUL WHAT YOU WISH FOR, FOR DANGER COULD BE JUST AROUND THE CORNER.
THAT'S REALLY MORE OF A PROVERB THAN A RIDDLE.
I'D SAY ADAGE.
I MUST GO!
Ka-boom
"AROUND THE CORNER." WHAT COULD IT MEAN?

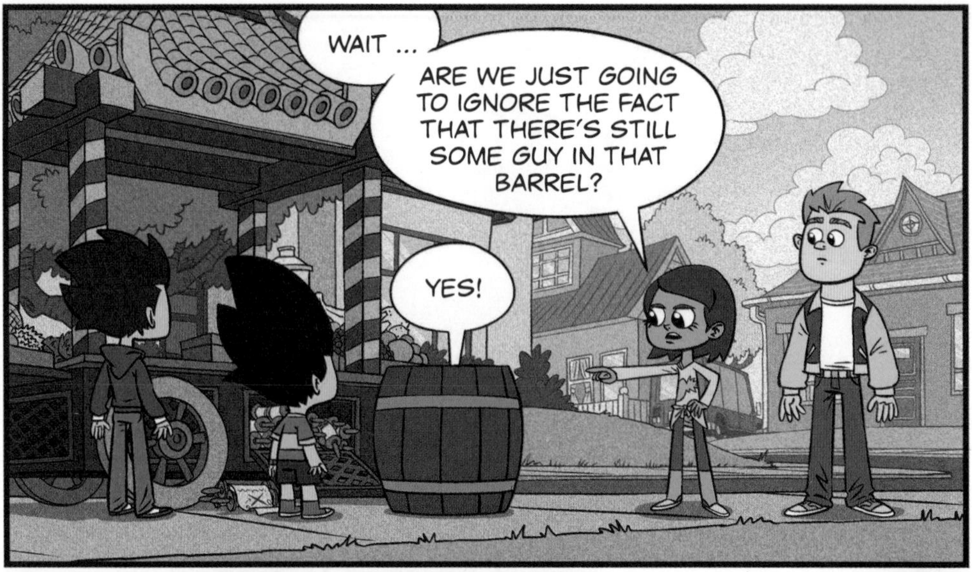
WAIT ...
ARE WE JUST GOING TO IGNORE THE FACT THAT THERE'S STILL SOME GUY IN THAT BARREL?
YES!

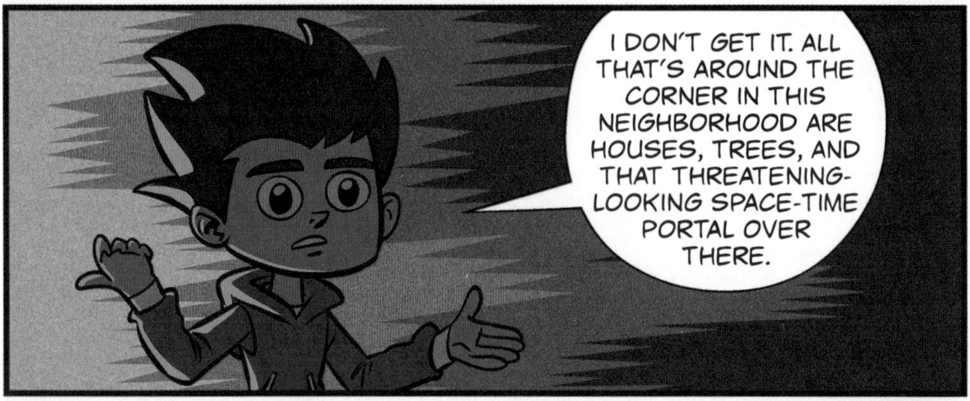
I DON'T GET IT. ALL THAT'S AROUND THE CORNER IN THIS NEIGHBORHOOD ARE HOUSES, TREES, AND THAT THREATENING-LOOKING SPACE-TIME PORTAL OVER THERE.

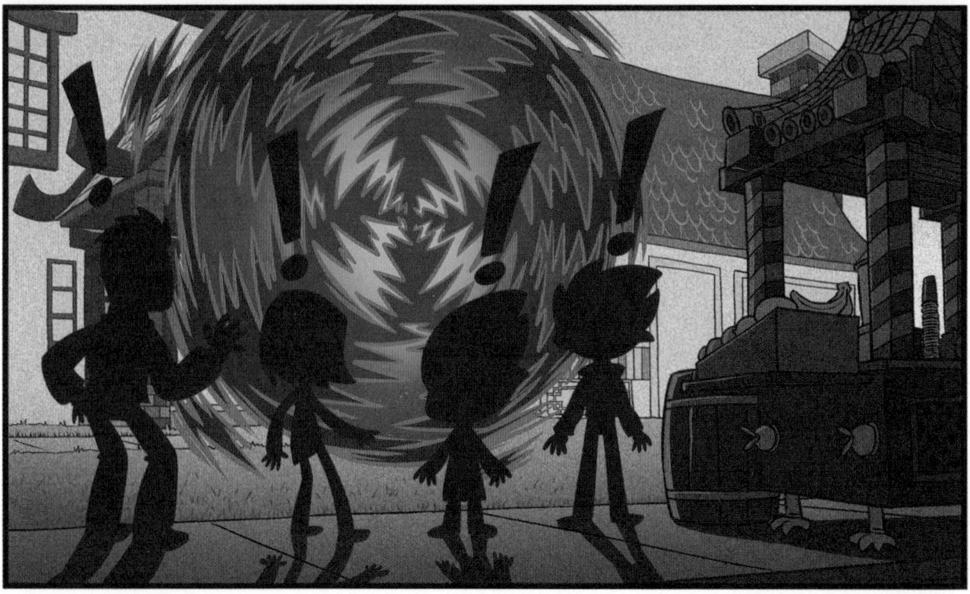

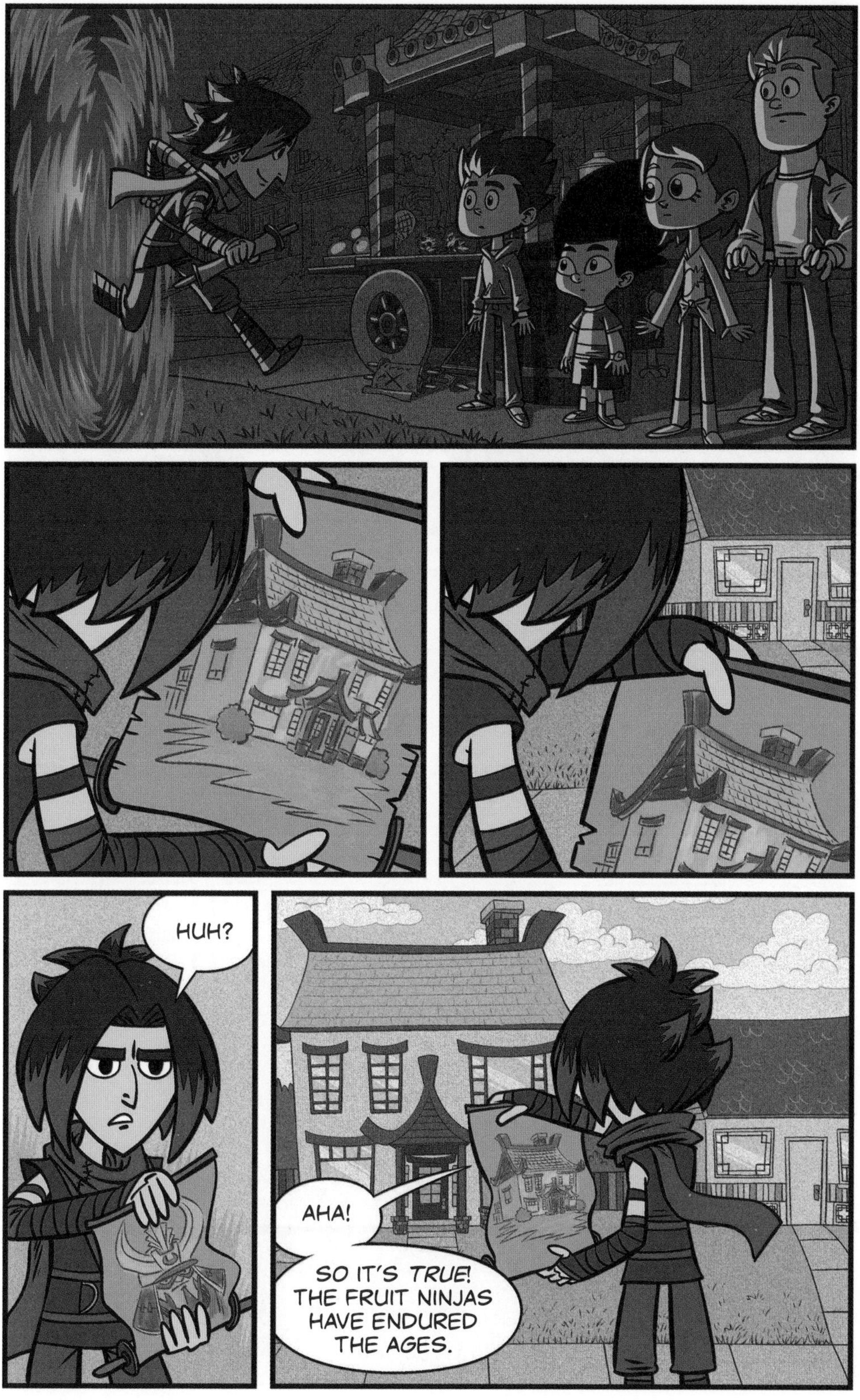
HUH?
AHA!
SO IT'S *TRUE*! THE FRUIT NINJAS HAVE ENDURED THE AGES.

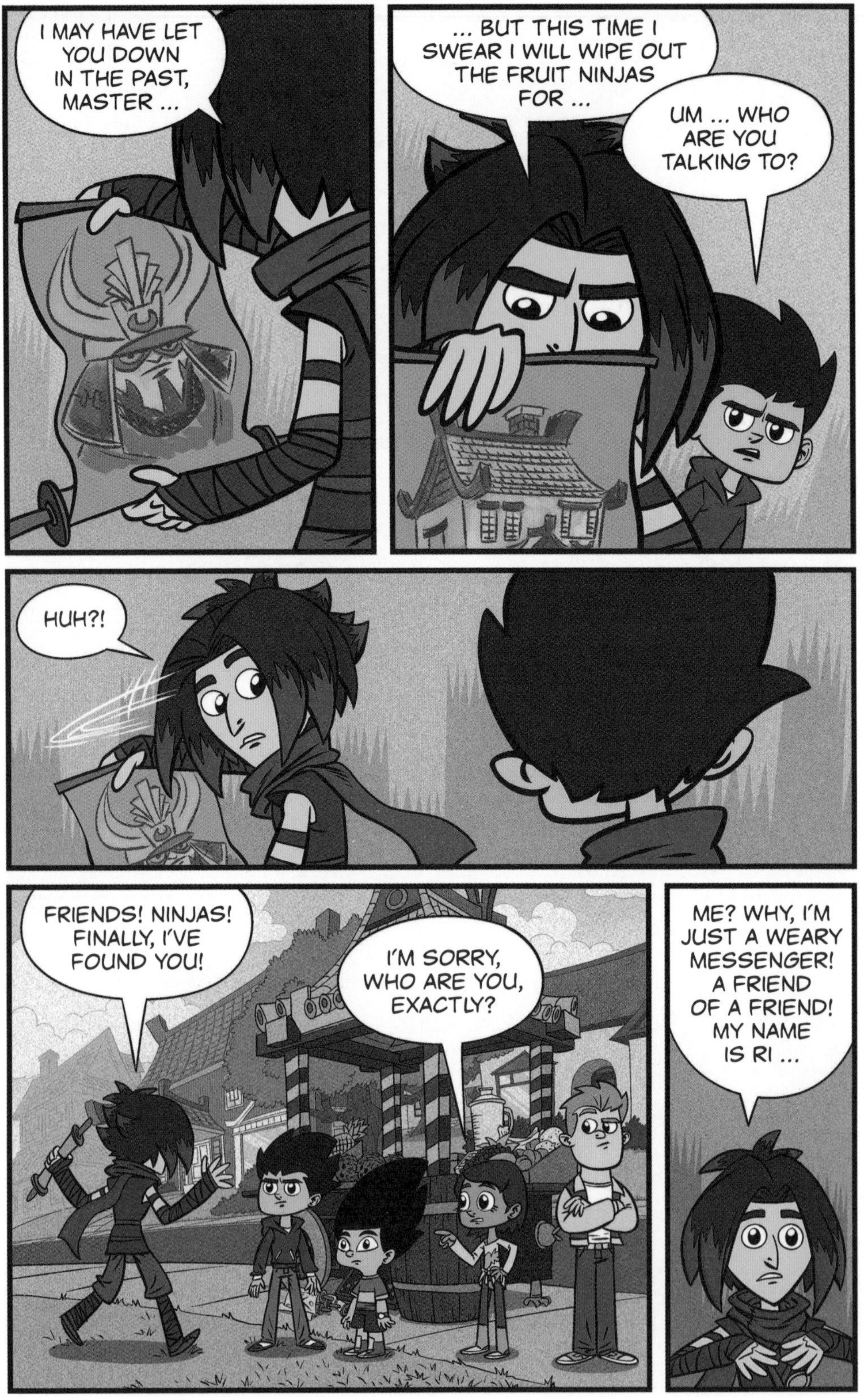
I MAY HAVE LET YOU DOWN IN THE PAST, MASTER ...
... BUT THIS TIME I SWEAR I WILL WIPE OUT THE FRUIT NINJAS FOR ...
UM ... WHO ARE YOU TALKING TO?
HUH?!
FRIENDS! NINJAS! FINALLY, I'VE FOUND YOU!
I'M SORRY, WHO ARE YOU, EXACTLY?
ME? WHY, I'M JUST A WEARY MESSENGER! A FRIEND OF A FRIEND! MY NAME IS RI ...

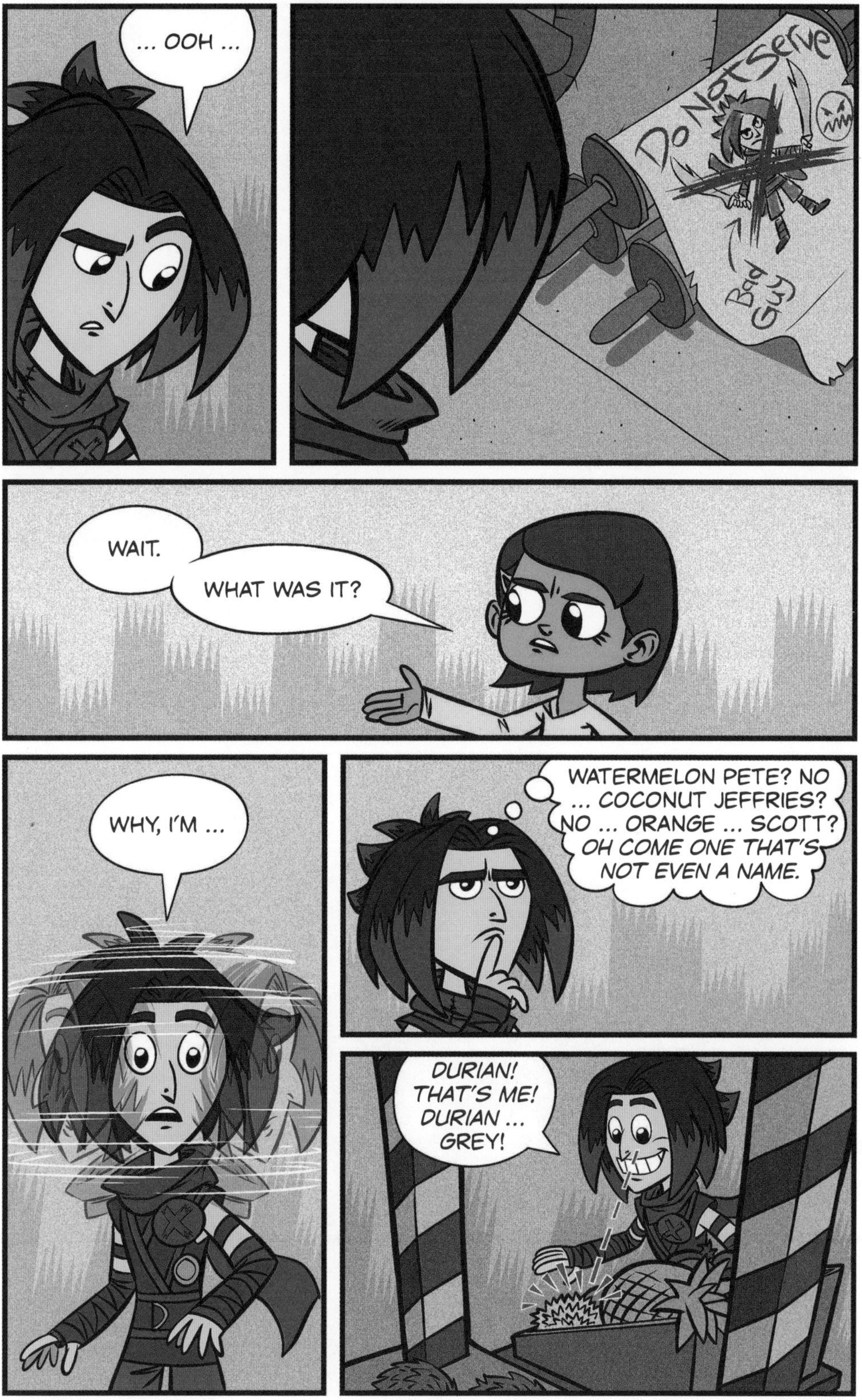
... OOH ...
Do Not serve
Bad Guy
WAIT.
WHAT WAS IT?
WHY, I'M ...
WATERMELON PETE? NO ... COCONUT JEFFRIES? NO ... ORANGE ... SCOTT? OH COME ONE THAT'S NOT EVEN A NAME.
DURIAN! THAT'S ME! DURIAN ... GREY!

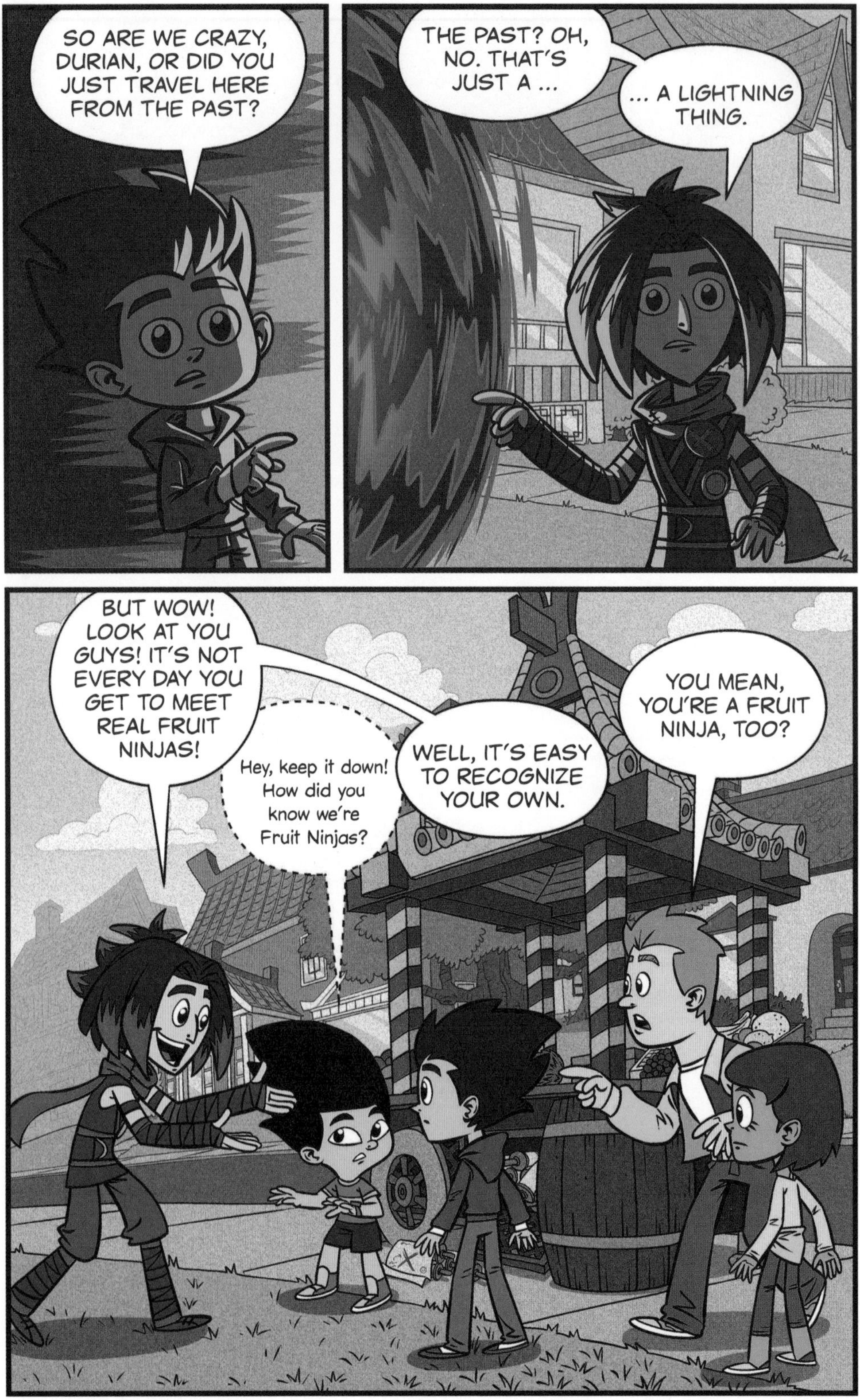
SO ARE WE CRAZY, DURIAN, OR DID YOU JUST TRAVEL HERE FROM THE PAST?
THE PAST? OH, NO. THAT'S JUST A ...
... A LIGHTNING THING.
BUT WOW! LOOK AT YOU GUYS! IT'S NOT EVERY DAY YOU GET TO MEET REAL FRUIT NINJAS!
Hey, keep it down! How did you know we're Fruit Ninjas?
WELL, IT'S EASY TO RECOGNIZE YOUR OWN.
YOU MEAN, YOU'RE A FRUIT NINJA, TOO?

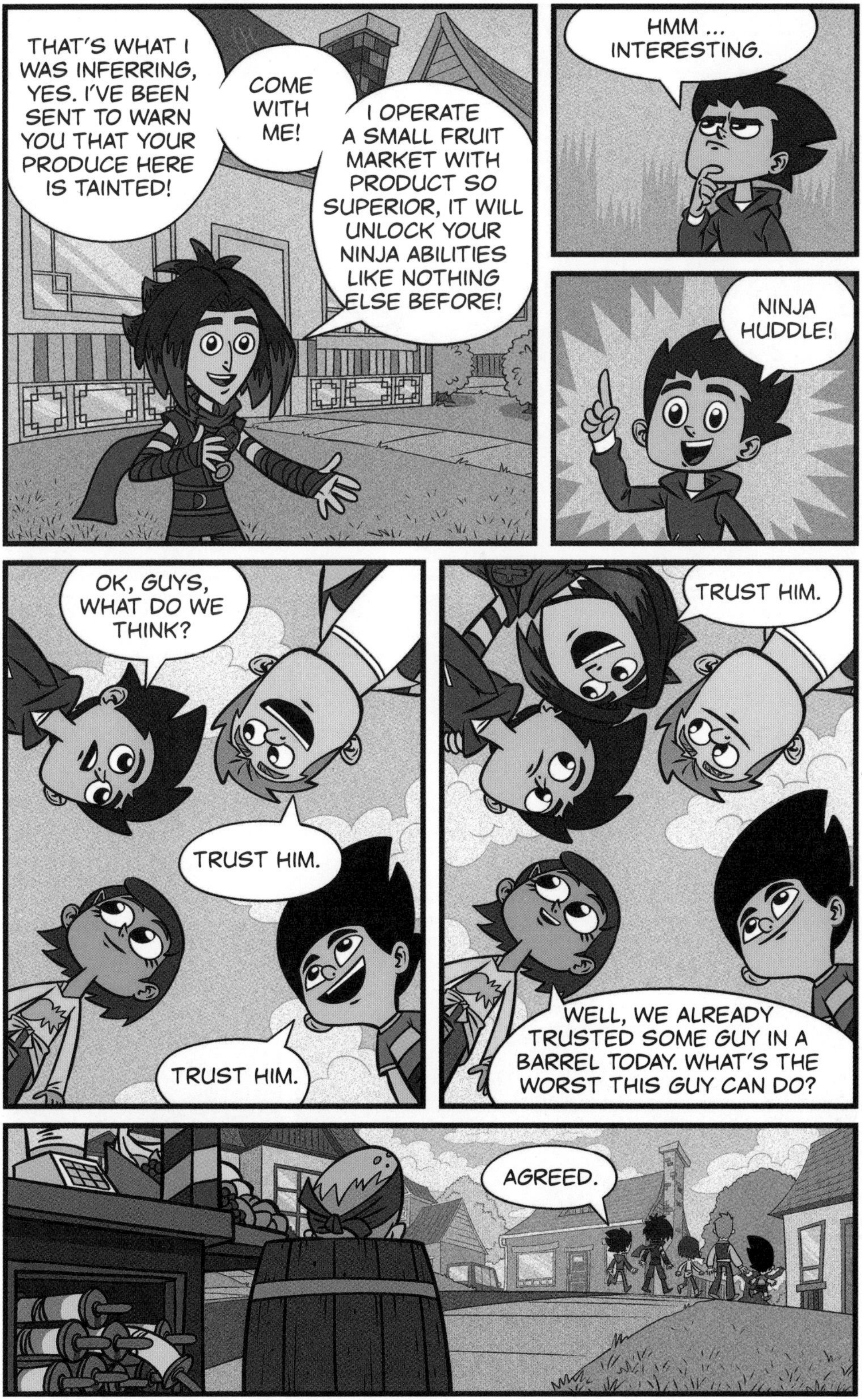
THAT'S WHAT I WAS INFERRING, YES. I'VE BEEN SENT TO WARN YOU THAT YOUR PRODUCE HERE IS TAINTED!
COME WITH ME!
I OPERATE A SMALL FRUIT MARKET WITH PRODUCT SO SUPERIOR, IT WILL UNLOCK YOUR NINJA ABILITIES LIKE NOTHING ELSE BEFORE!
HMM ... INTERESTING.
NINJA HUDDLE!
OK, GUYS, WHAT DO WE THINK?
TRUST HIM.
TRUST HIM.
TRUST HIM.
WELL, WE ALREADY TRUSTED SOME GUY IN A BARREL TODAY. WHAT'S THE WORST THIS GUY CAN DO?
AGREED.

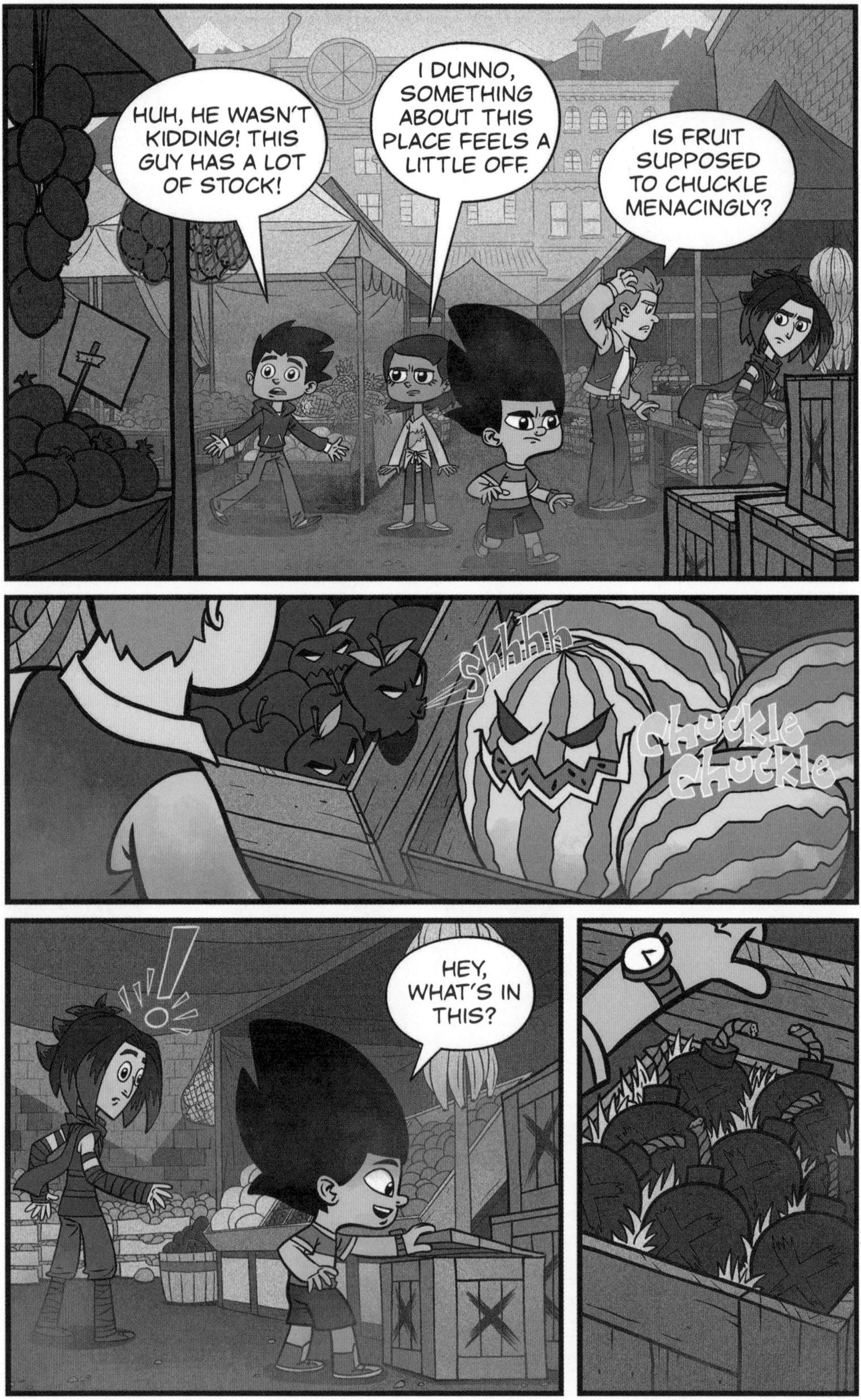
HUH, HE WASN'T KIDDING! THIS GUY HAS A LOT OF STOCK!
I DUNNO, SOMETHING ABOUT THIS PLACE FEELS A LITTLE OFF.
IS FRUIT SUPPOSED TO CHUCKLE MENACINGLY?
Shhhh
Chuckle Chuckle
!
HEY, WHAT'S IN THIS?

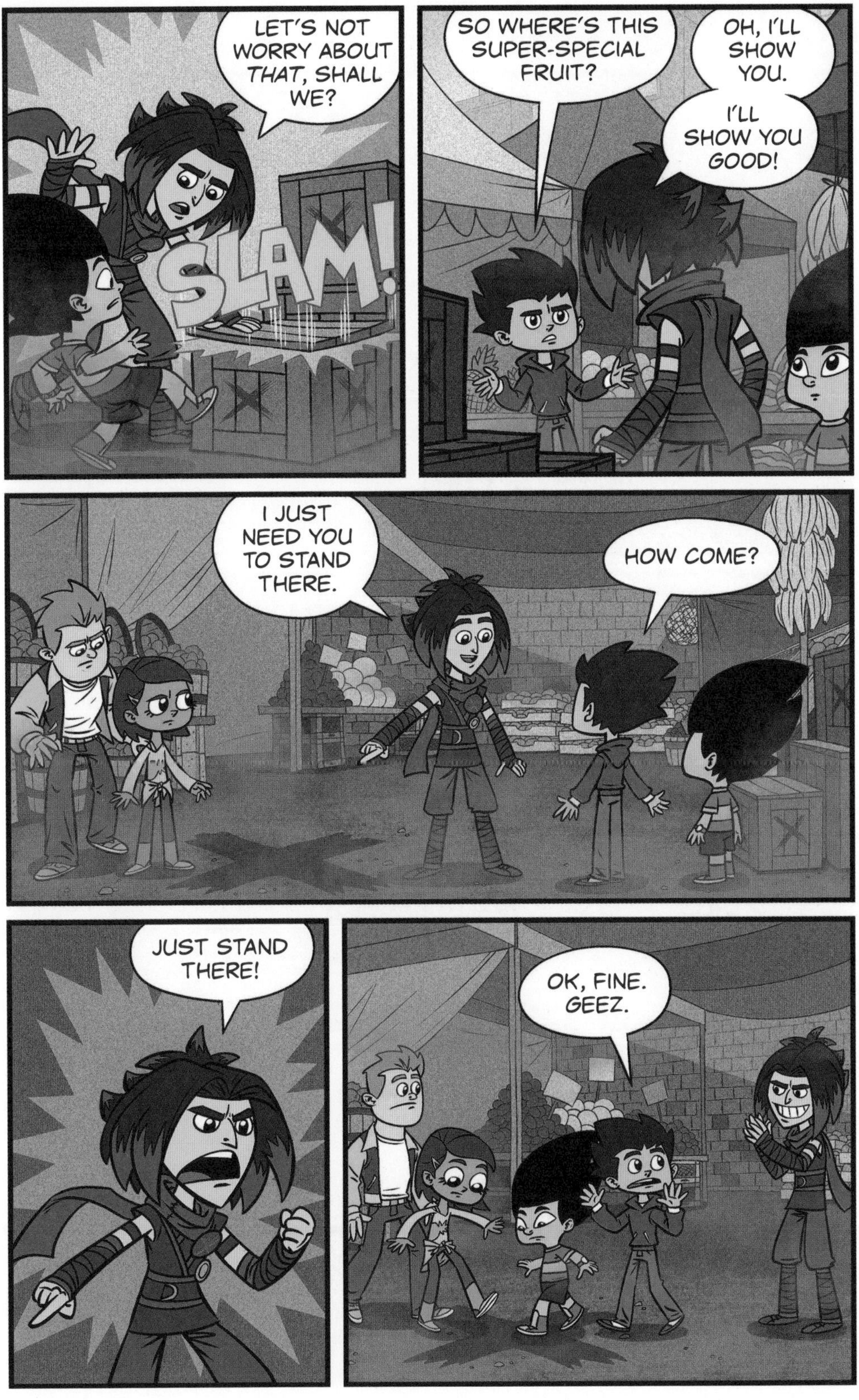
LET'S NOT WORRY ABOUT *THAT*, SHALL WE?
SLAM!
SO WHERE'S THIS SUPER-SPECIAL FRUIT?
OH, I'LL SHOW YOU.
I'LL SHOW YOU GOOD!
I JUST NEED YOU TO STAND THERE.
HOW COME?
JUST STAND THERE!
OK, FINE. GEEZ.

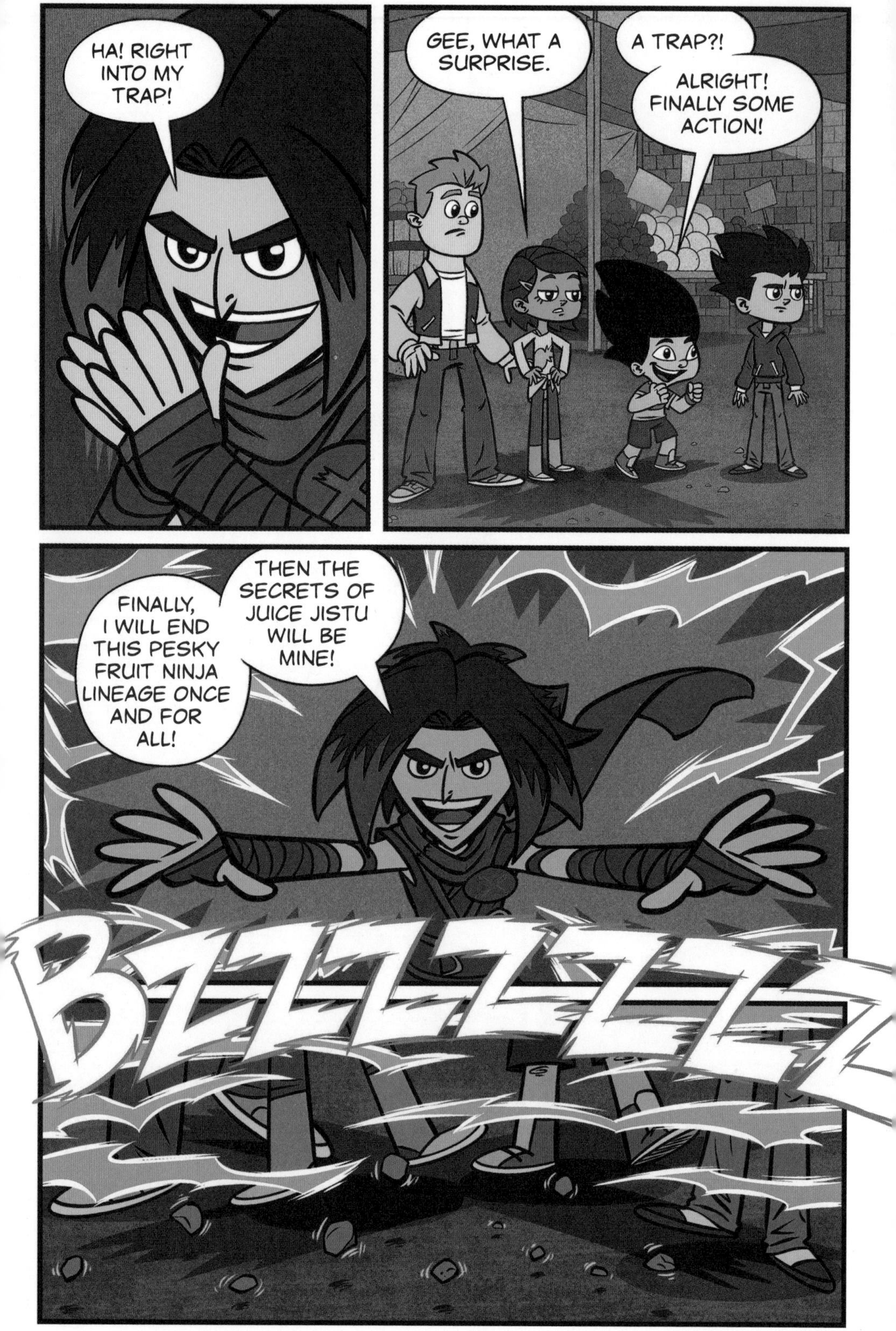
HA! RIGHT INTO MY TRAP!
GEE, WHAT A SURPRISE.
A TRAP?!
ALRIGHT! FINALLY SOME ACTION!
FINALLY, I WILL END THIS PESKY FRUIT NINJA LINEAGE ONCE AND FOR ALL!
THEN THE SECRETS OF JUICE JISTU WILL BE MINE!
BZZZZZZZ

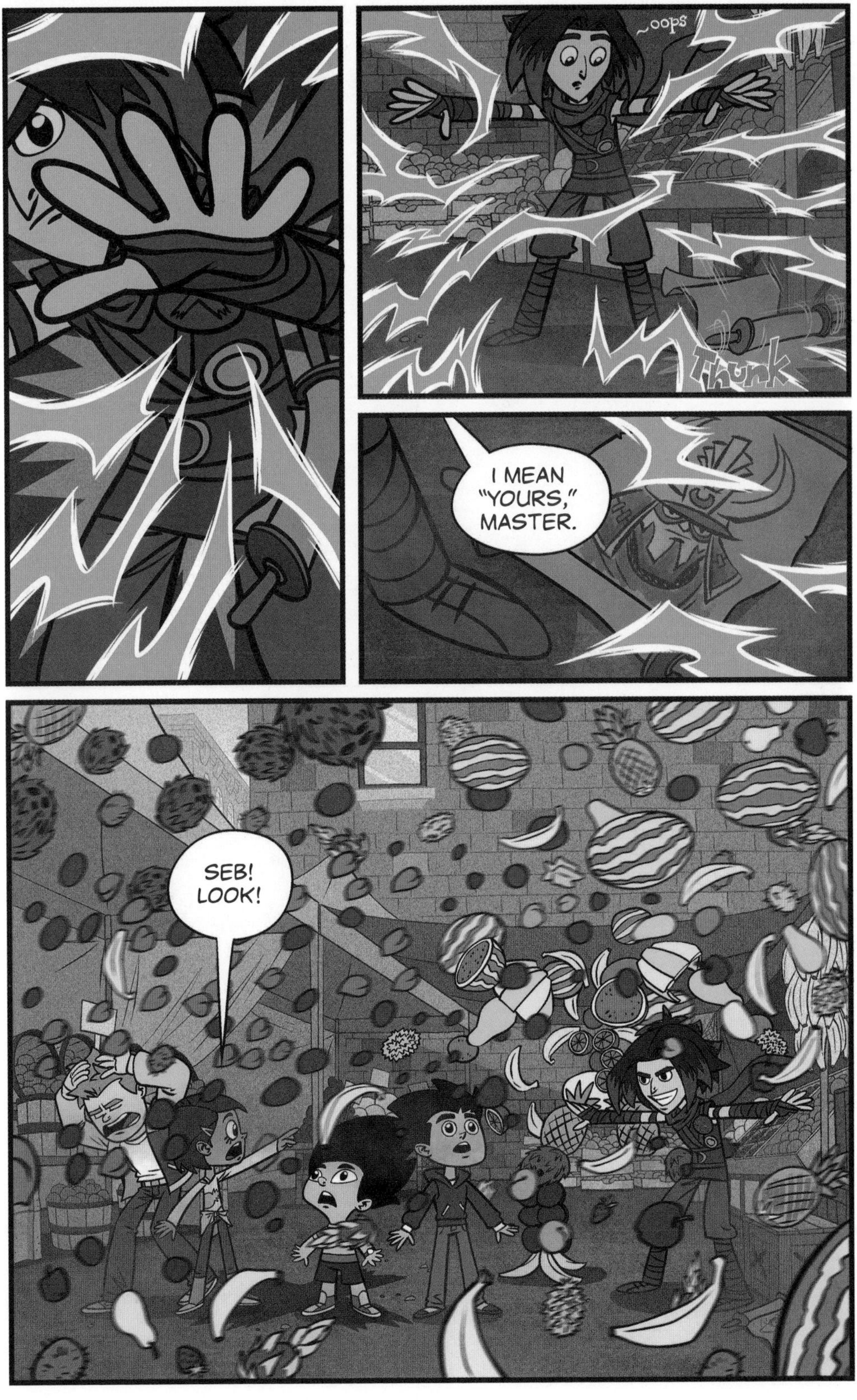
~oops
Thunk
I MEAN "YOURS," MASTER.
SEB! LOOK!

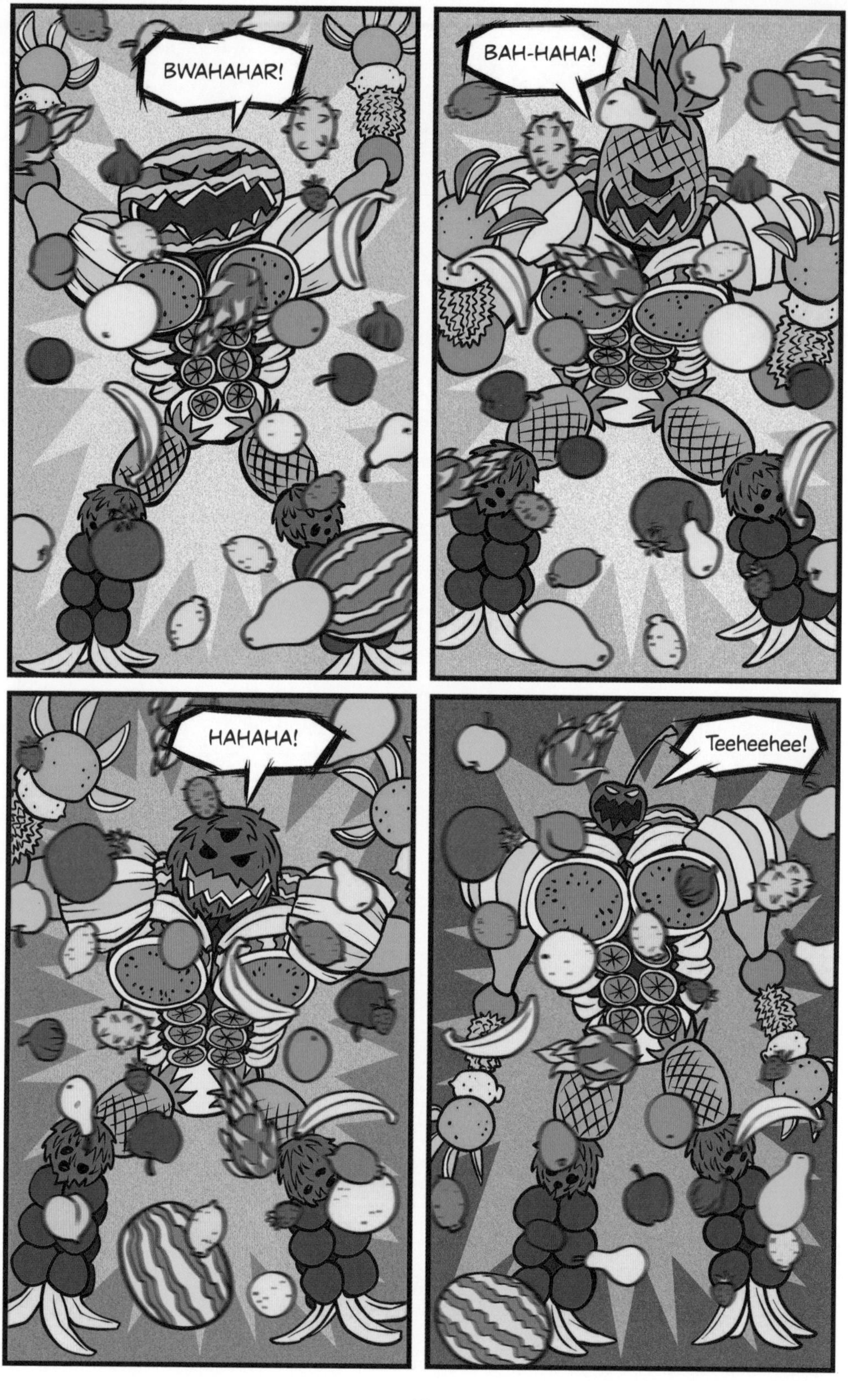
BWAHAHAR!
BAH-HAHA!
HAHAHA!
Teeheehee!

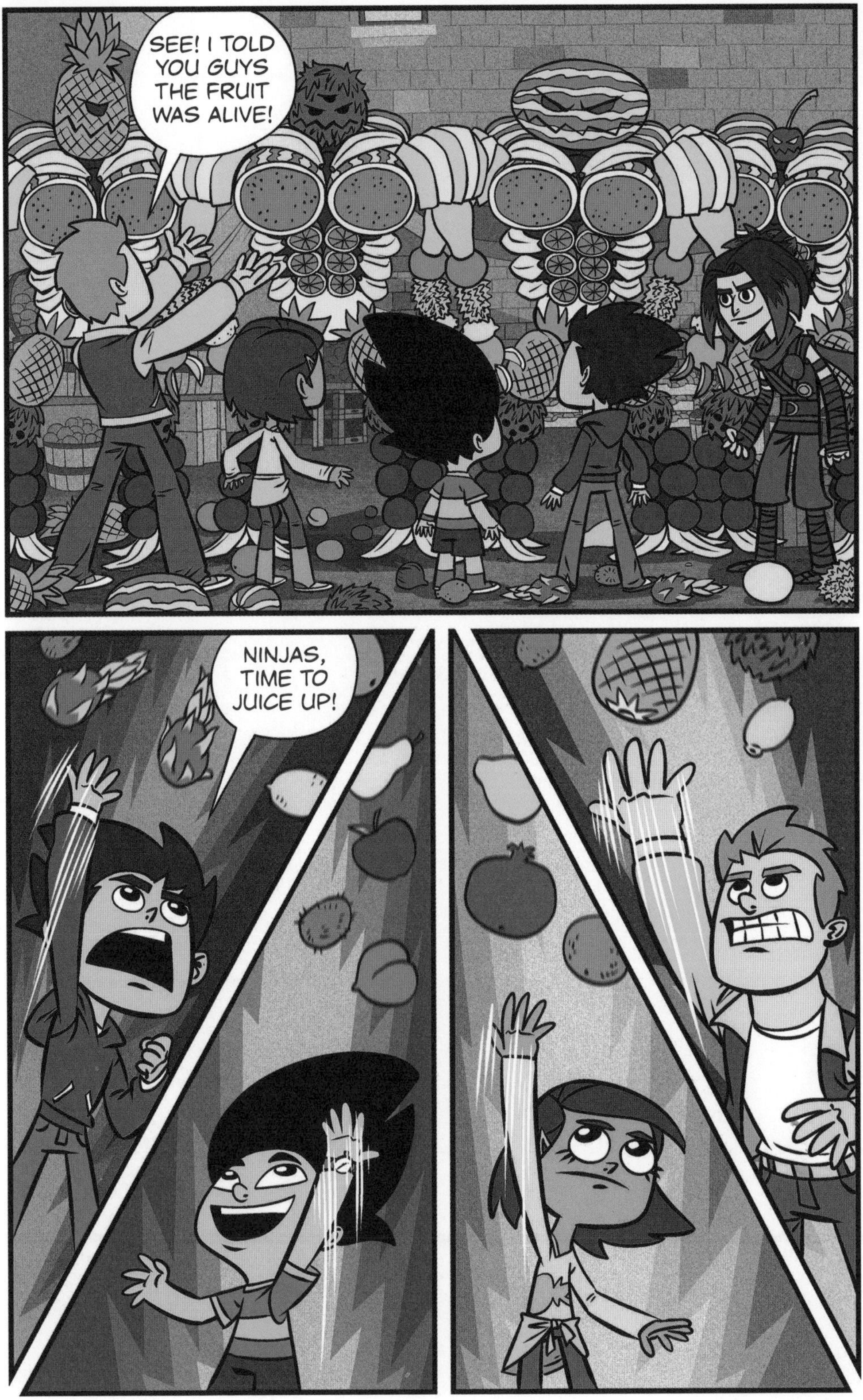
SEE! I TOLD YOU GUYS THE FRUIT WAS ALIVE!
NINJAS, TIME TO JUICE UP!

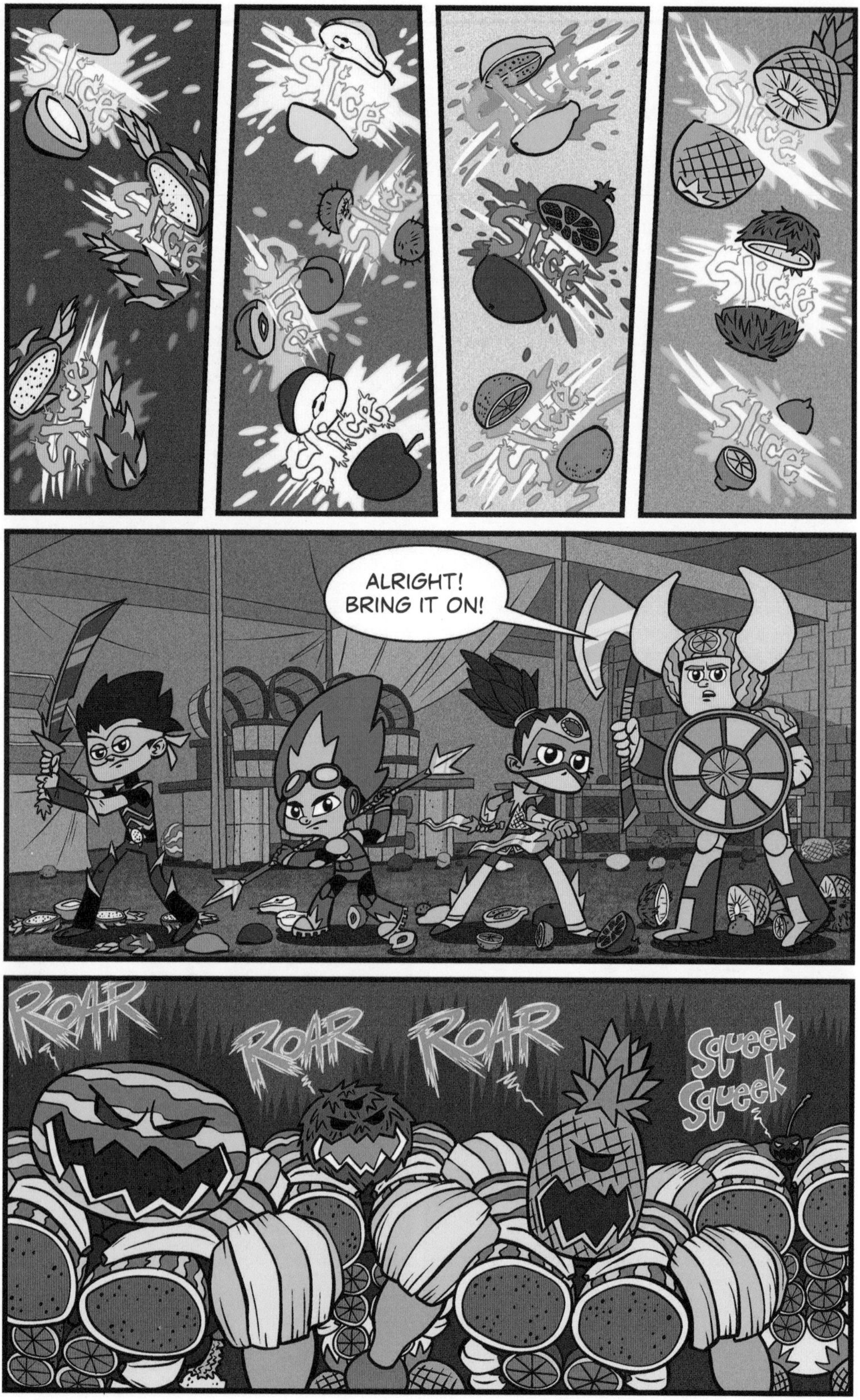
Slice
Slice
Slice
Slice
Slice
Slice
Slice
Slice
Slice
Slice
ALRIGHT! BRING IT ON!
ROAR
ROAR
ROAR
Squeek
Squeek

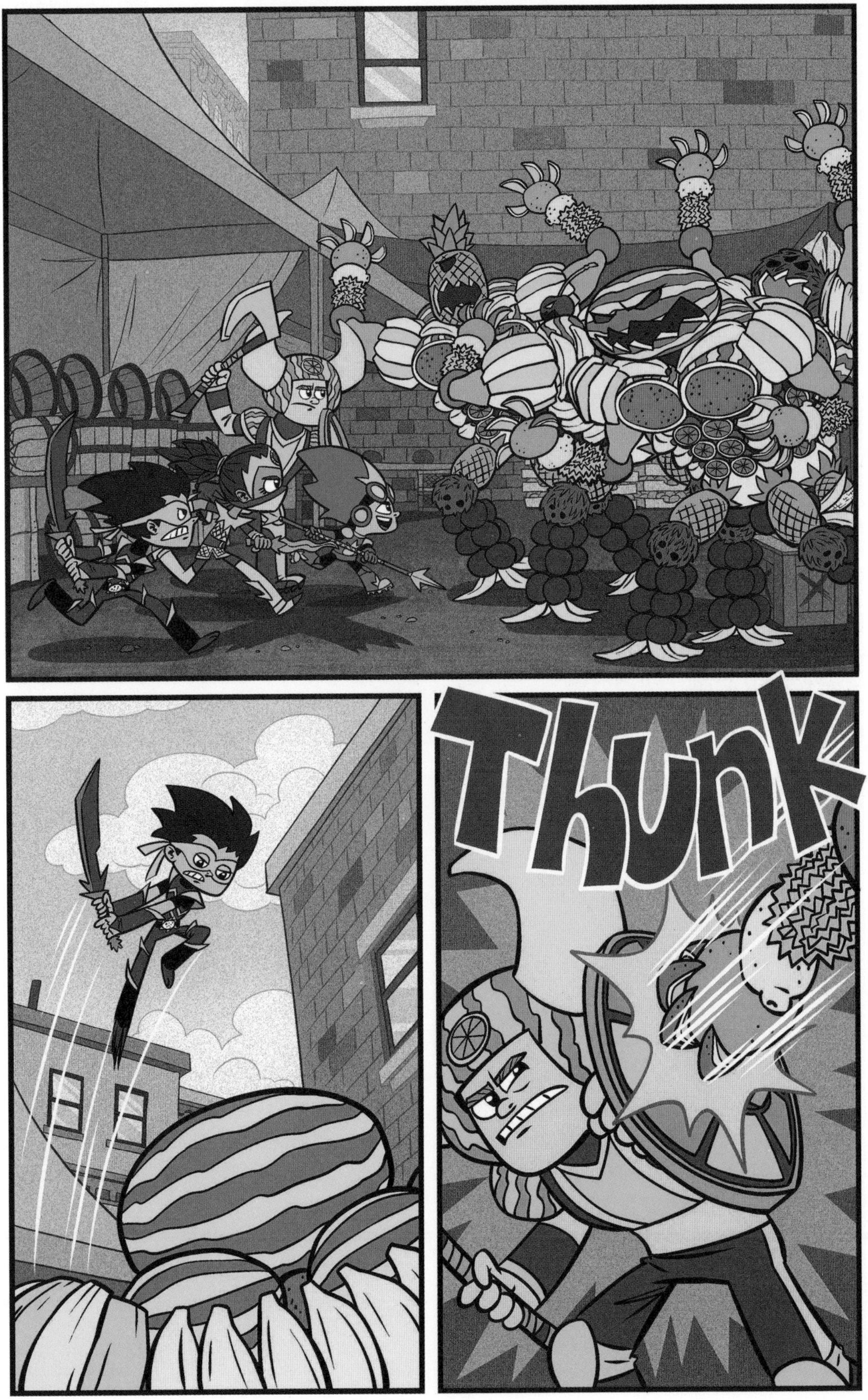
THUNK

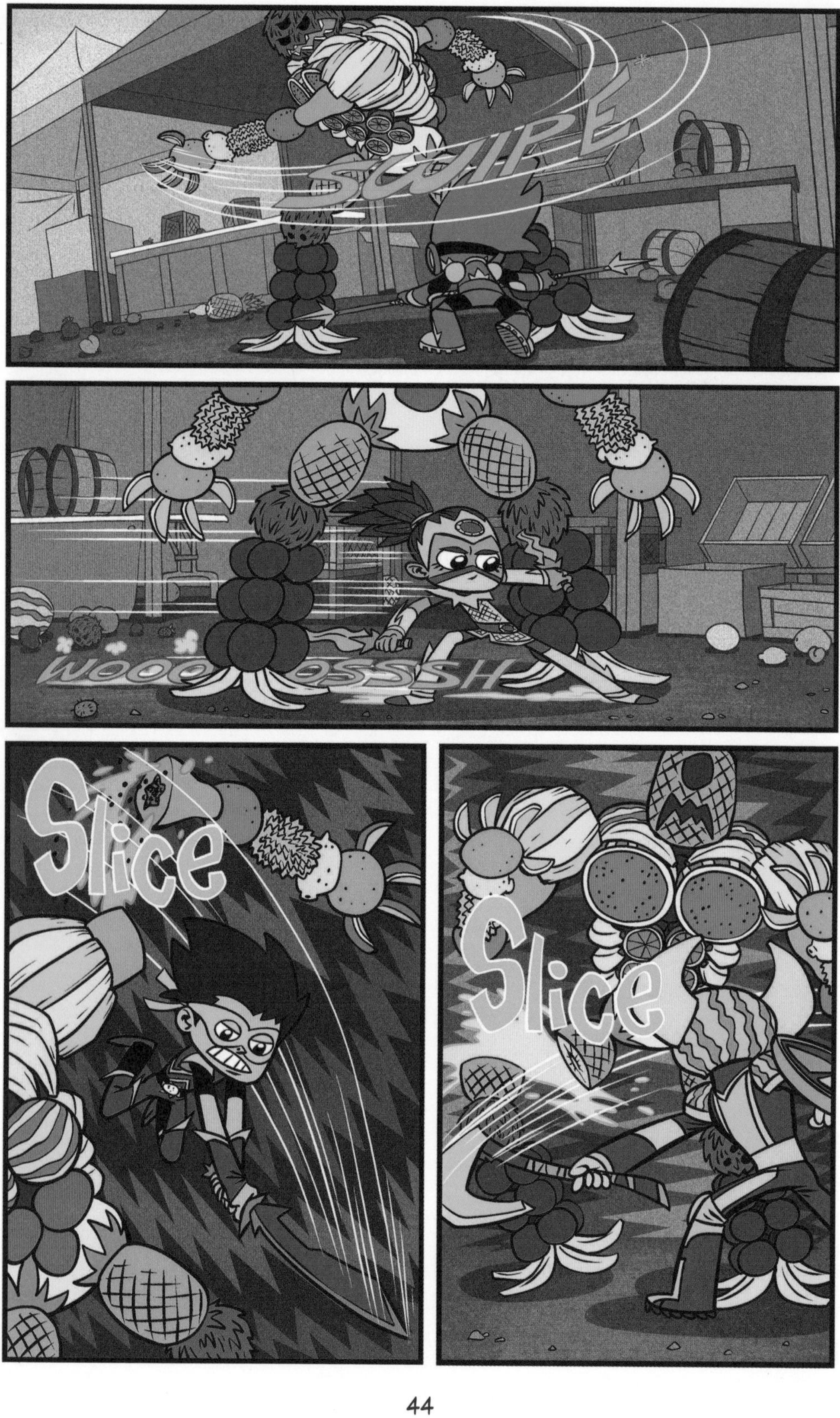
SWIPE*
WOOOOSSSH
Slice
Slice

* It totally missed

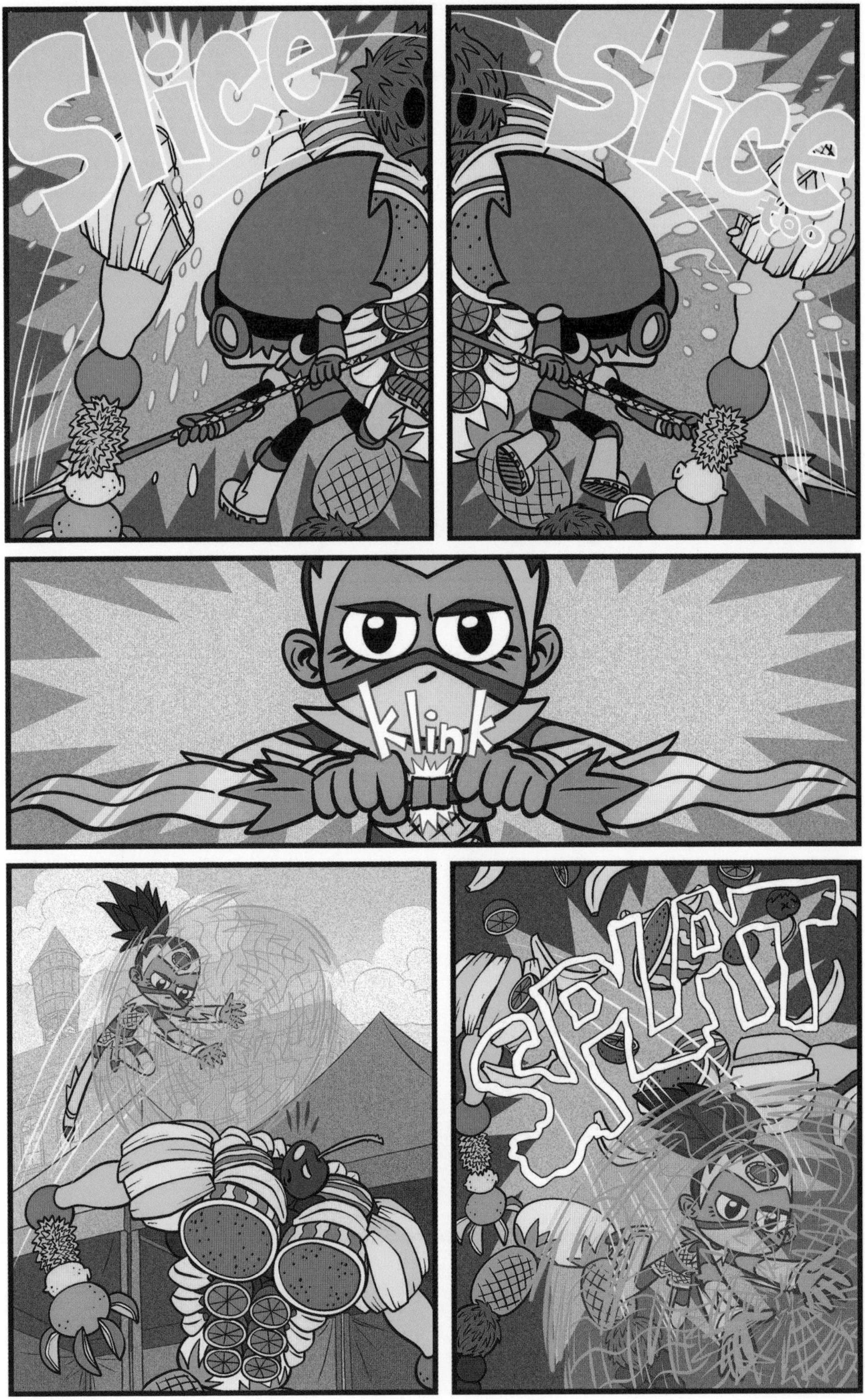
Slice
Slice too
klink

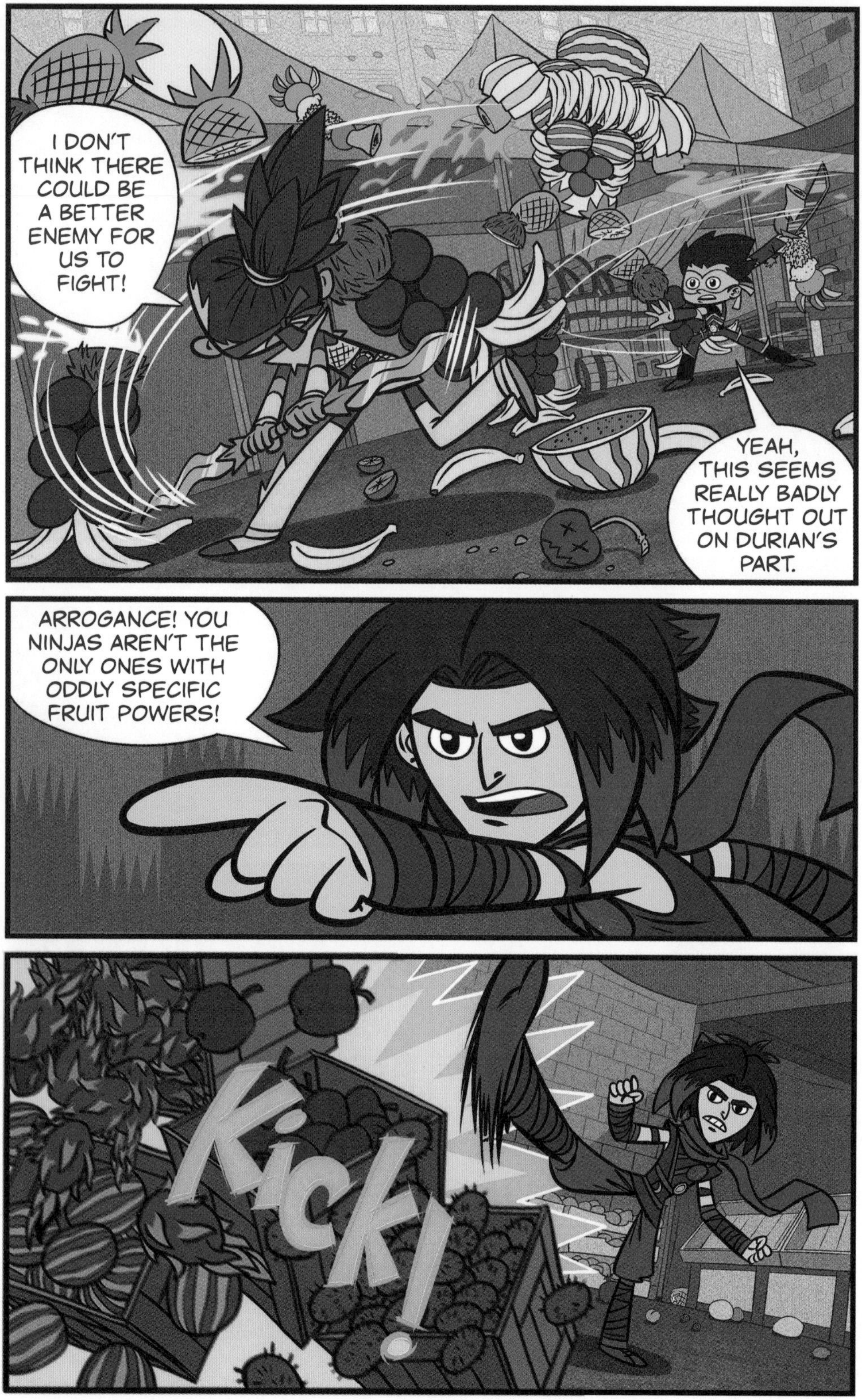
I DON'T THINK THERE COULD BE A BETTER ENEMY FOR US TO FIGHT!
YEAH, THIS SEEMS REALLY BADLY THOUGHT OUT ON DURIAN'S PART.
ARROGANCE! YOU NINJAS AREN'T THE ONLY ONES WITH ODDLY SPECIFIC FRUIT POWERS!
KICK!

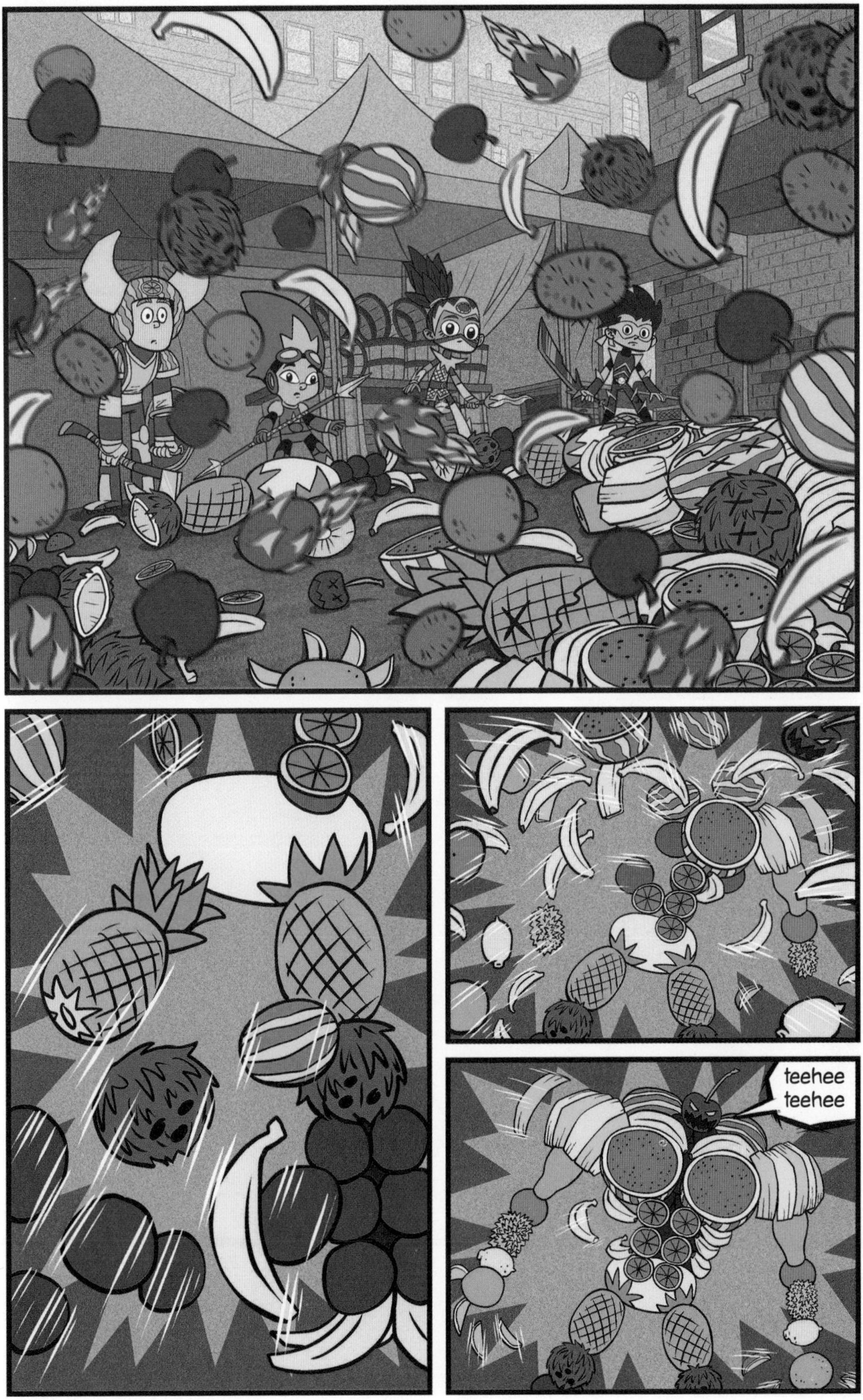
teehee
teehee

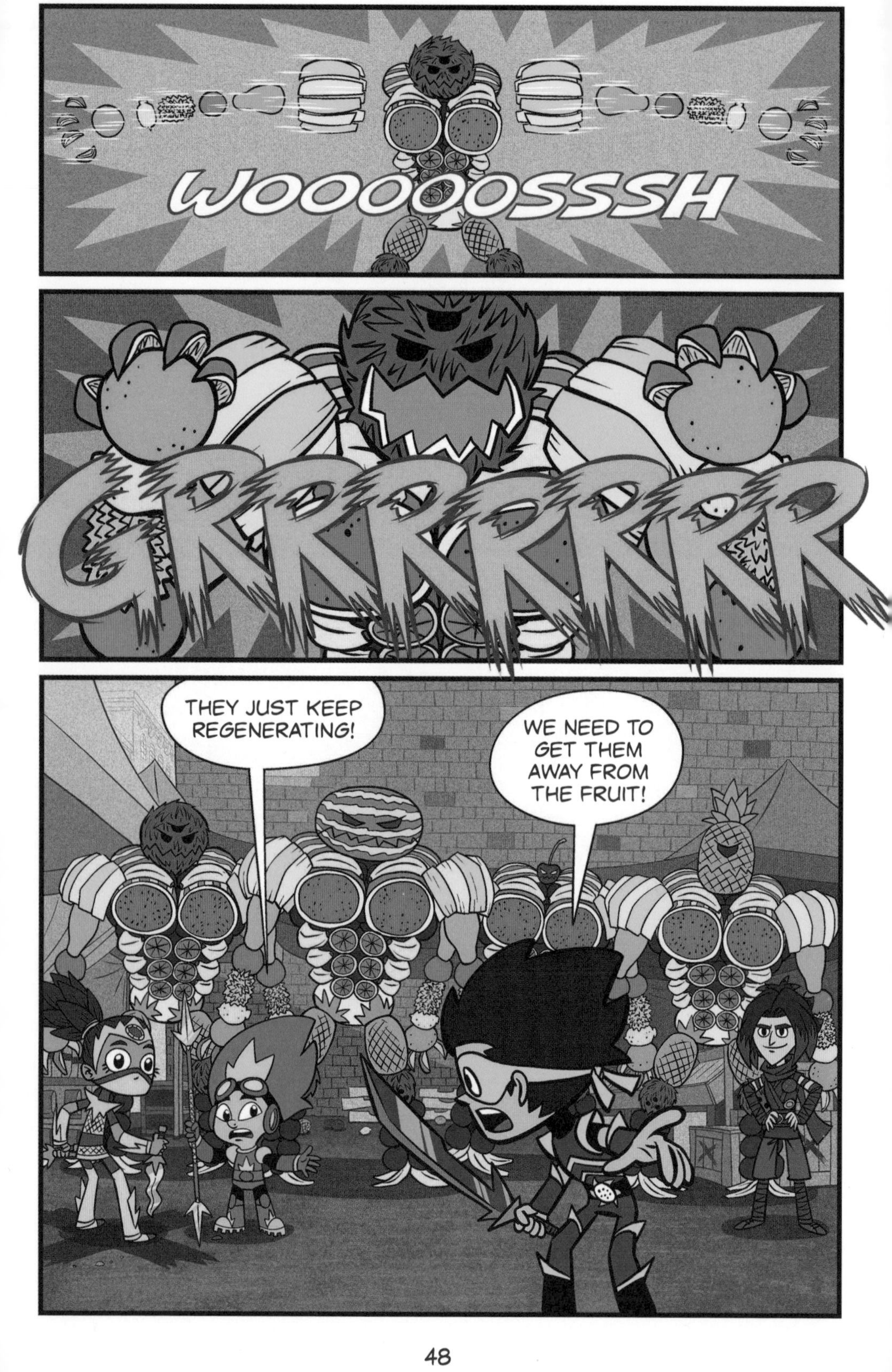
WOOOOOSSSSH
GRRRRRRR
THEY JUST KEEP REGENERATING!
WE NEED TO GET THEM AWAY FROM THE FRUIT!

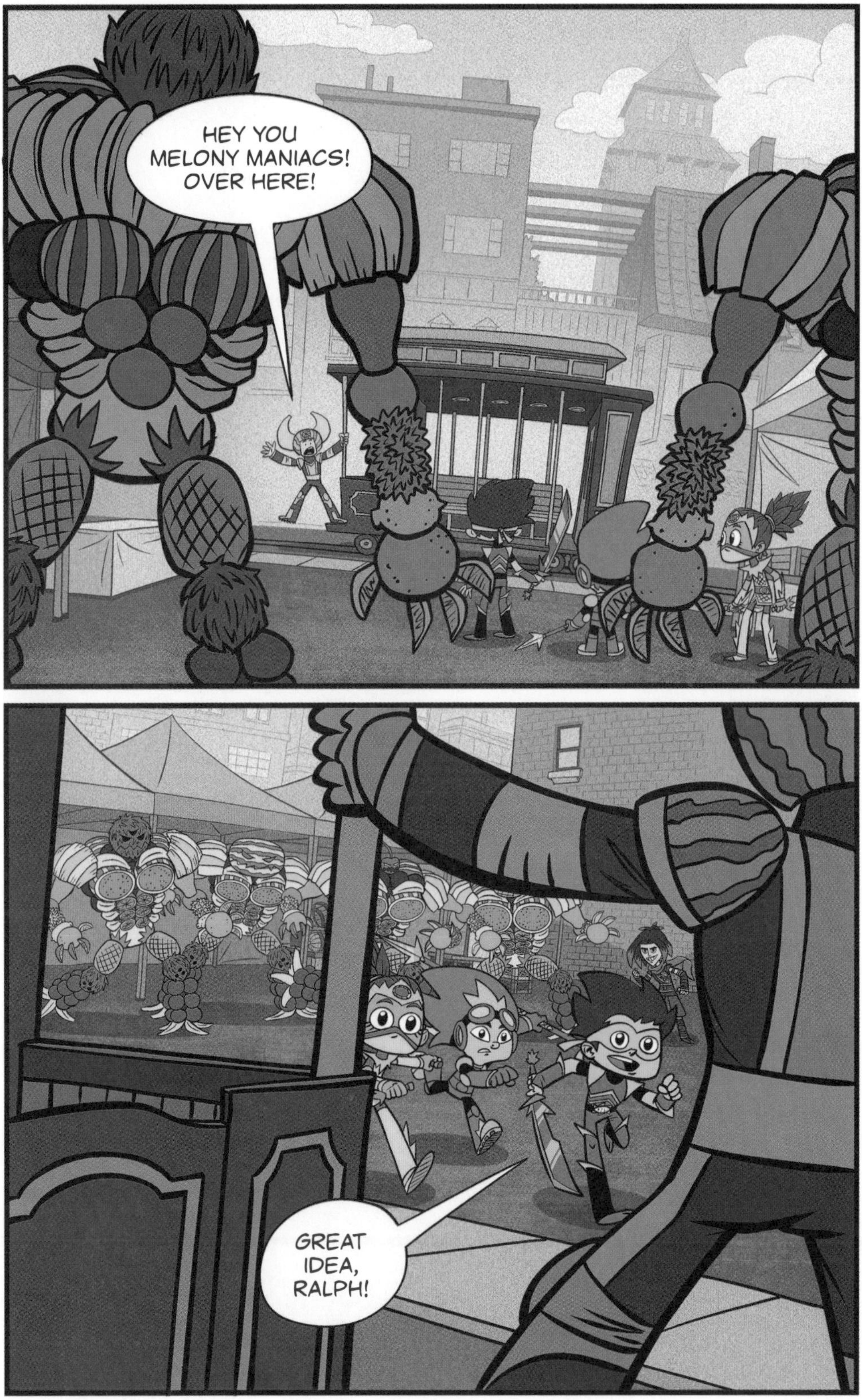
HEY YOU MELONY MANIACS! OVER HERE!
GREAT IDEA, RALPH!

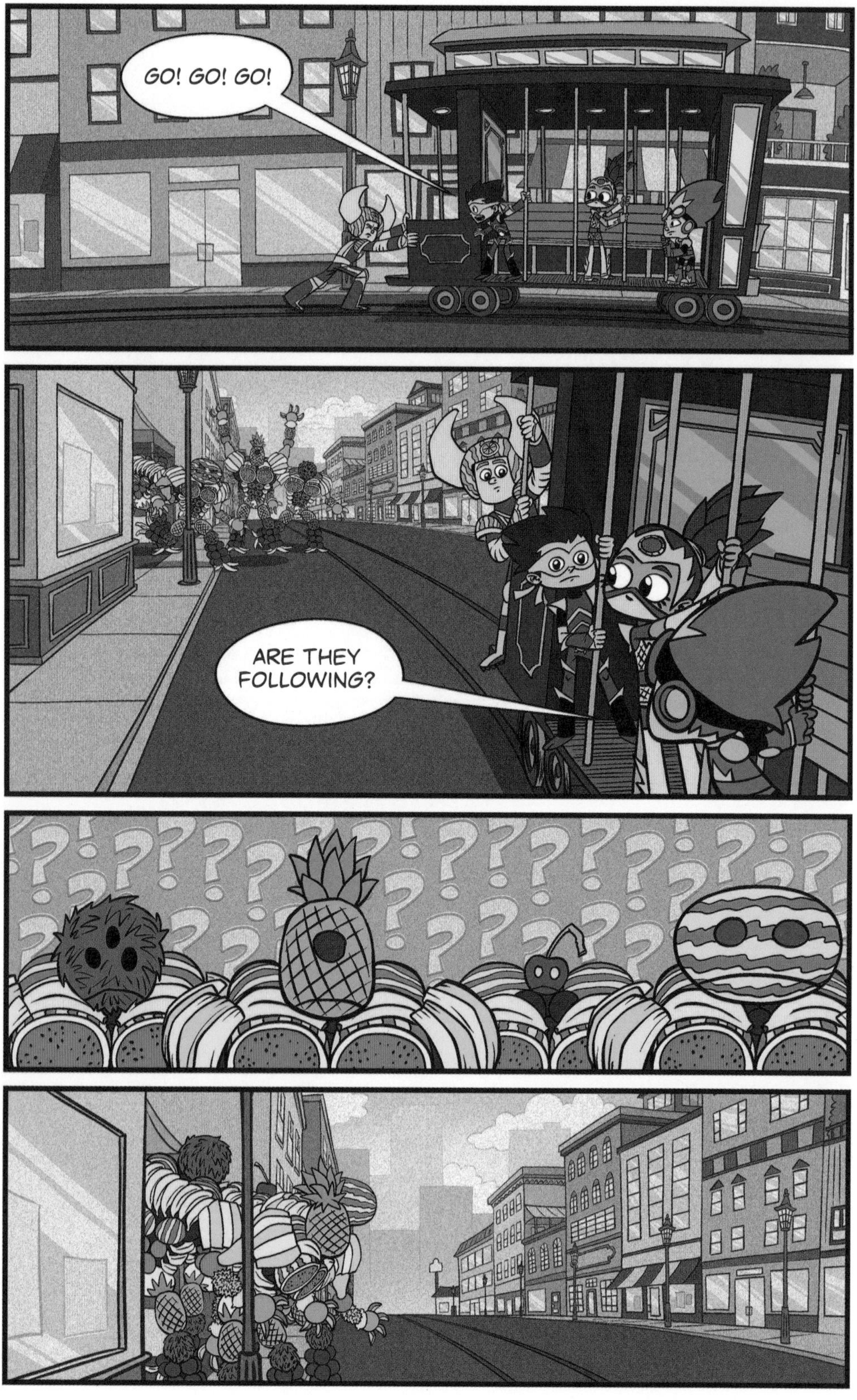
GO! GO! GO!
ARE THEY FOLLOWING?

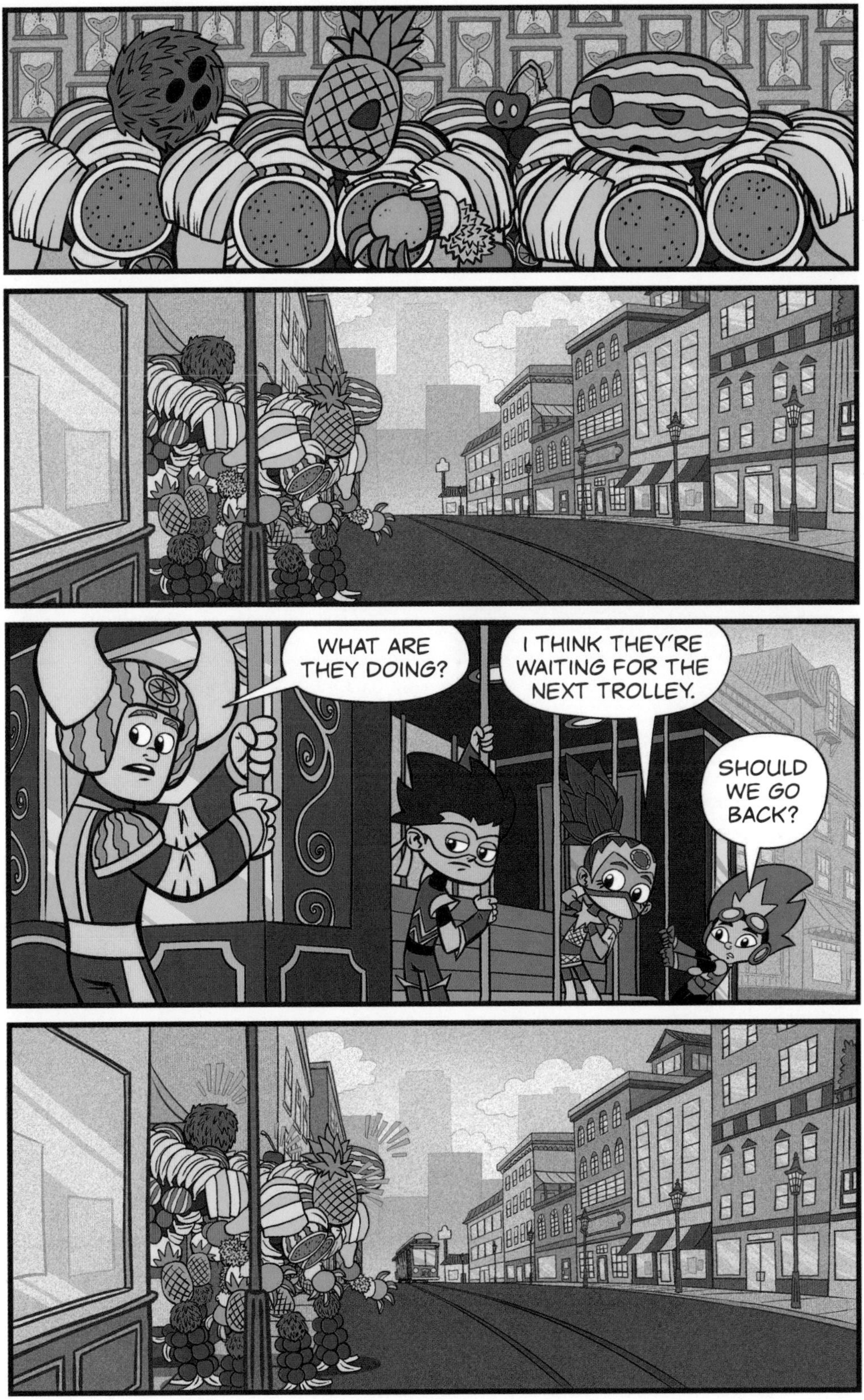
WHAT ARE THEY DOING?
I THINK THEY'RE WAITING FOR THE NEXT TROLLEY.
SHOULD WE GO BACK?

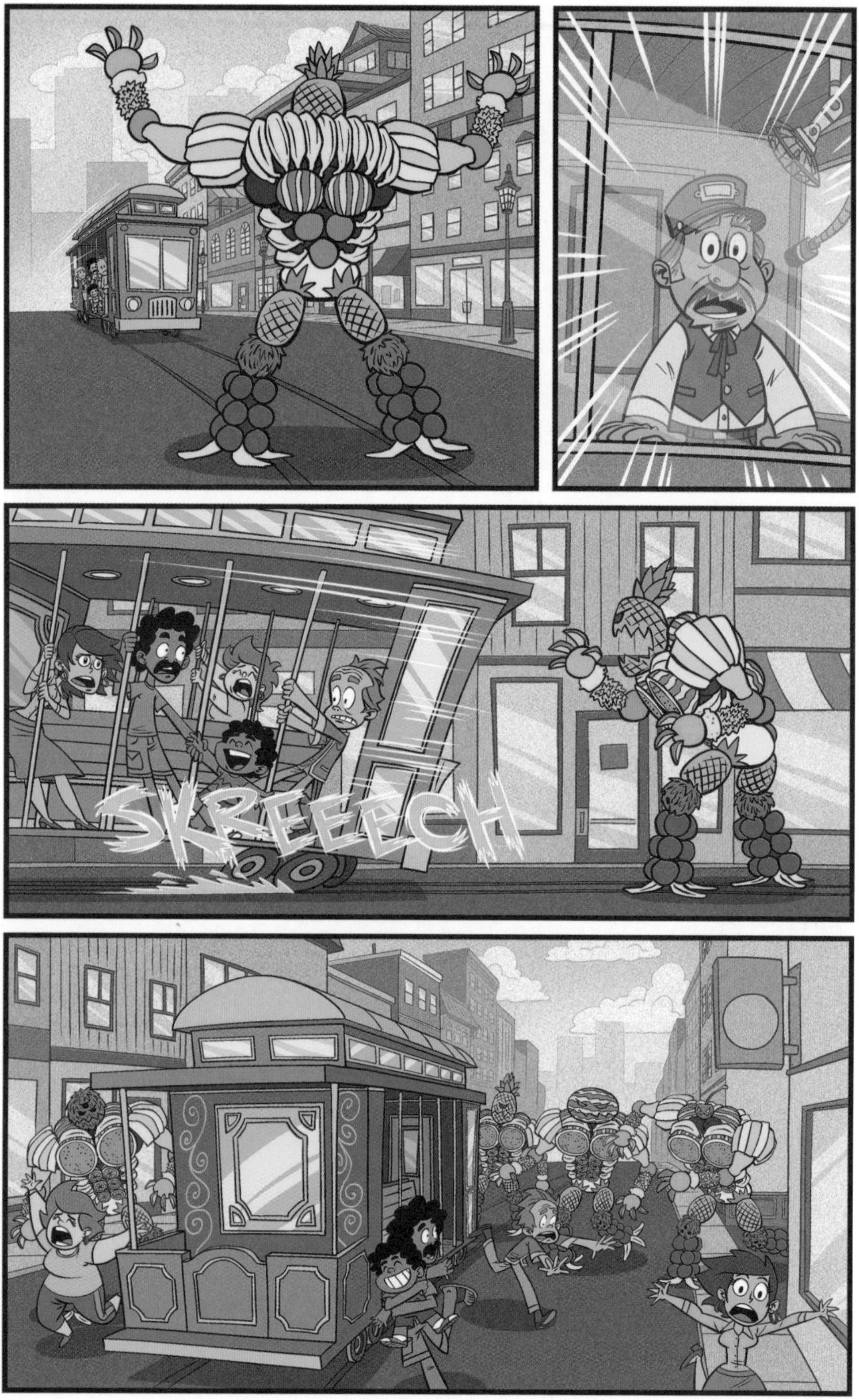
SKREEECH

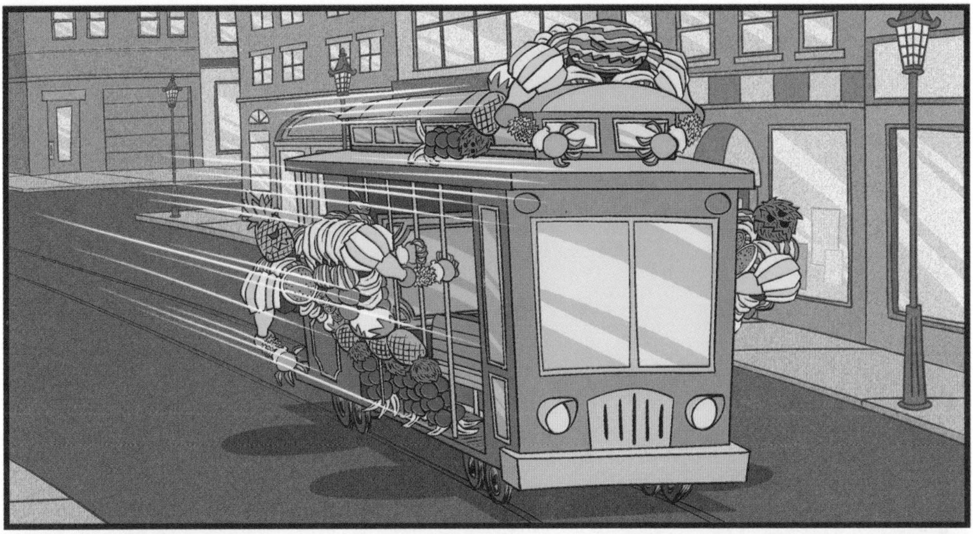

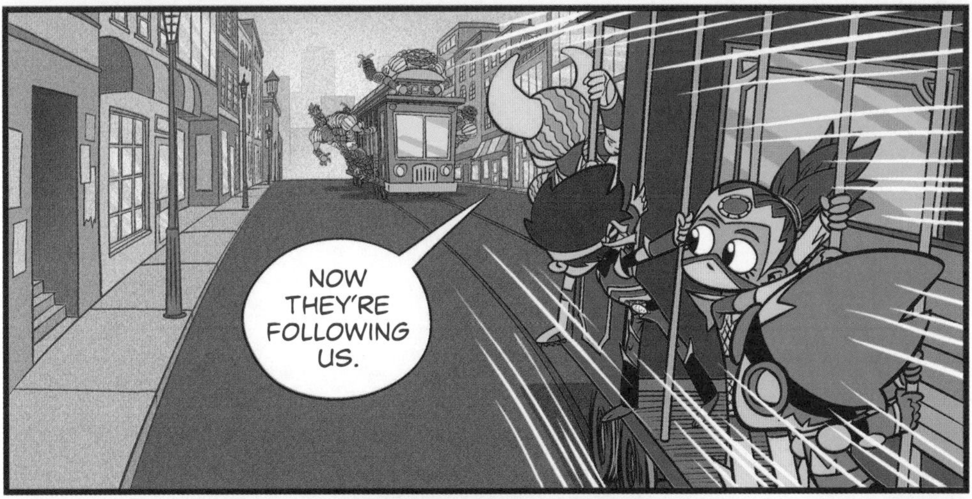
NOW THEY'RE FOLLOWING US.

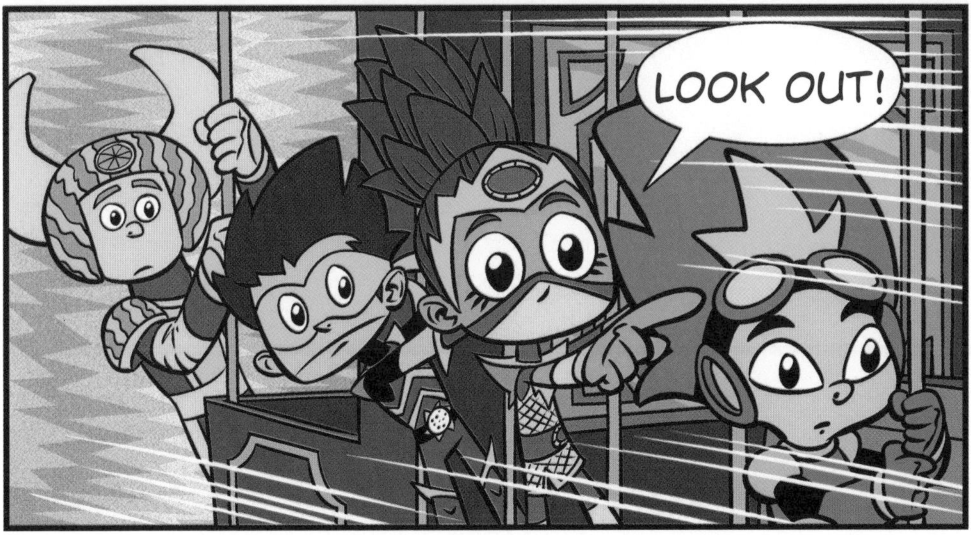
LOOK OUT!

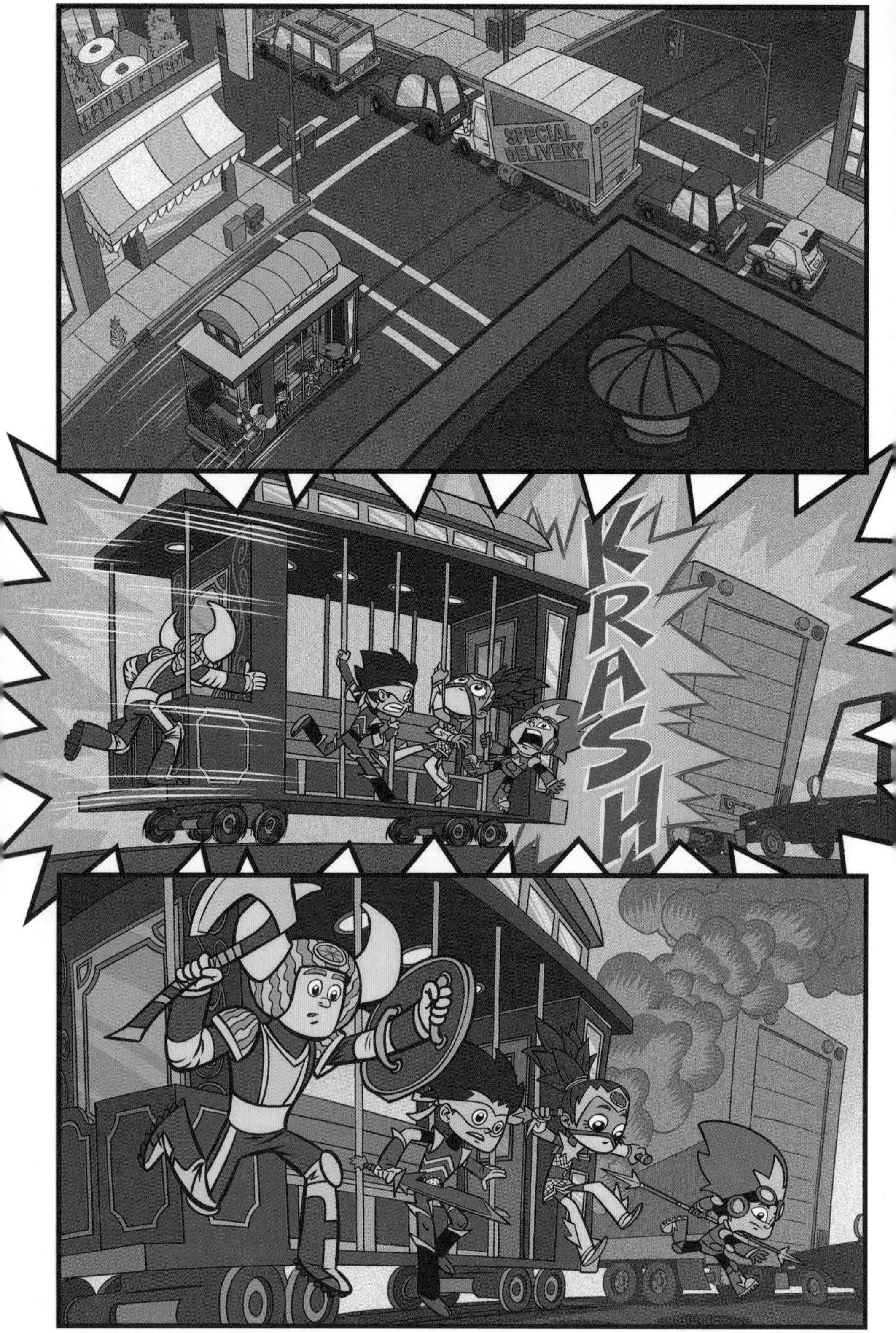
SPECIAL DELIVERY
KRASH

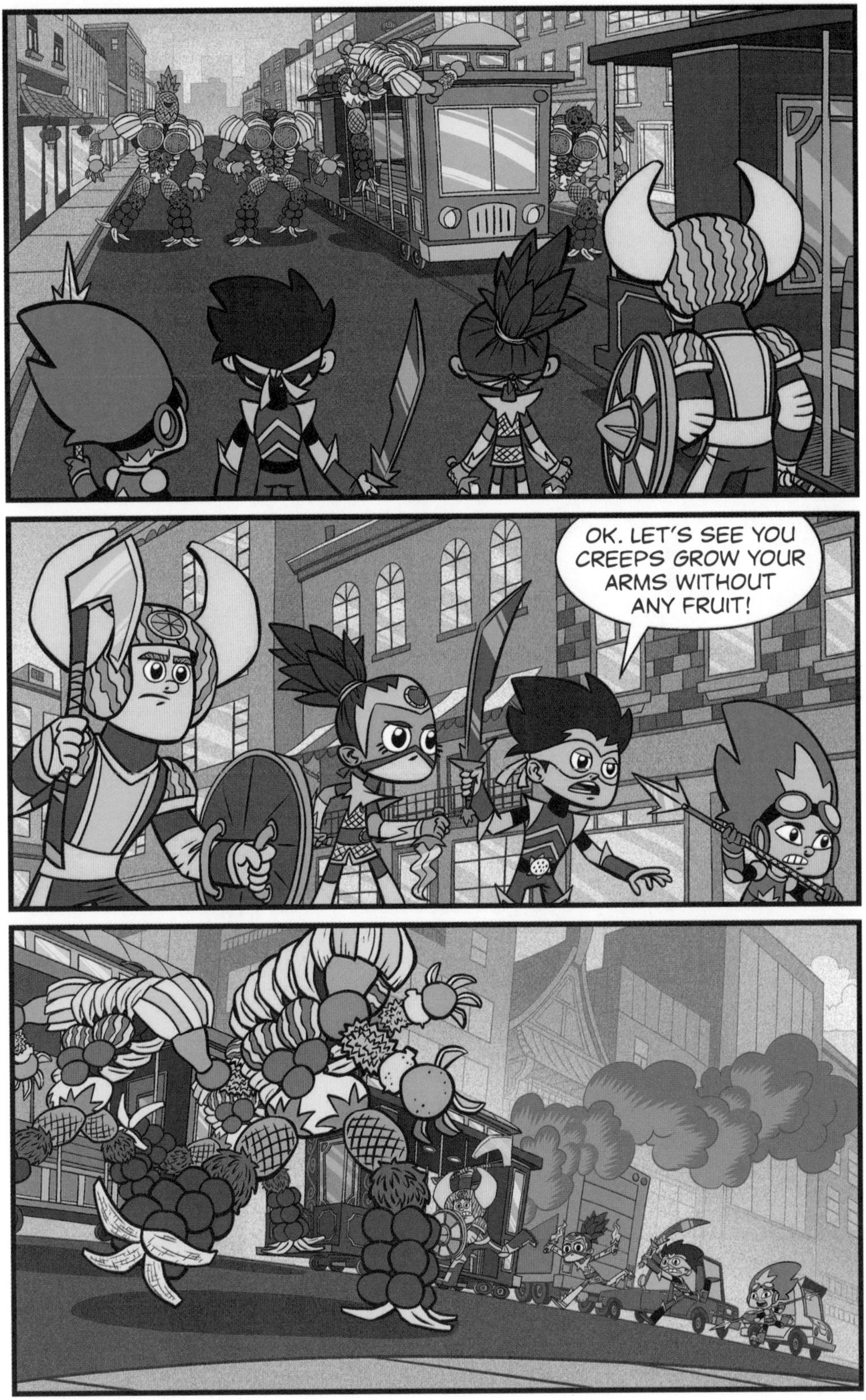
OK. LET'S SEE YOU CREEPS GROW YOUR ARMS WITHOUT ANY FRUIT!

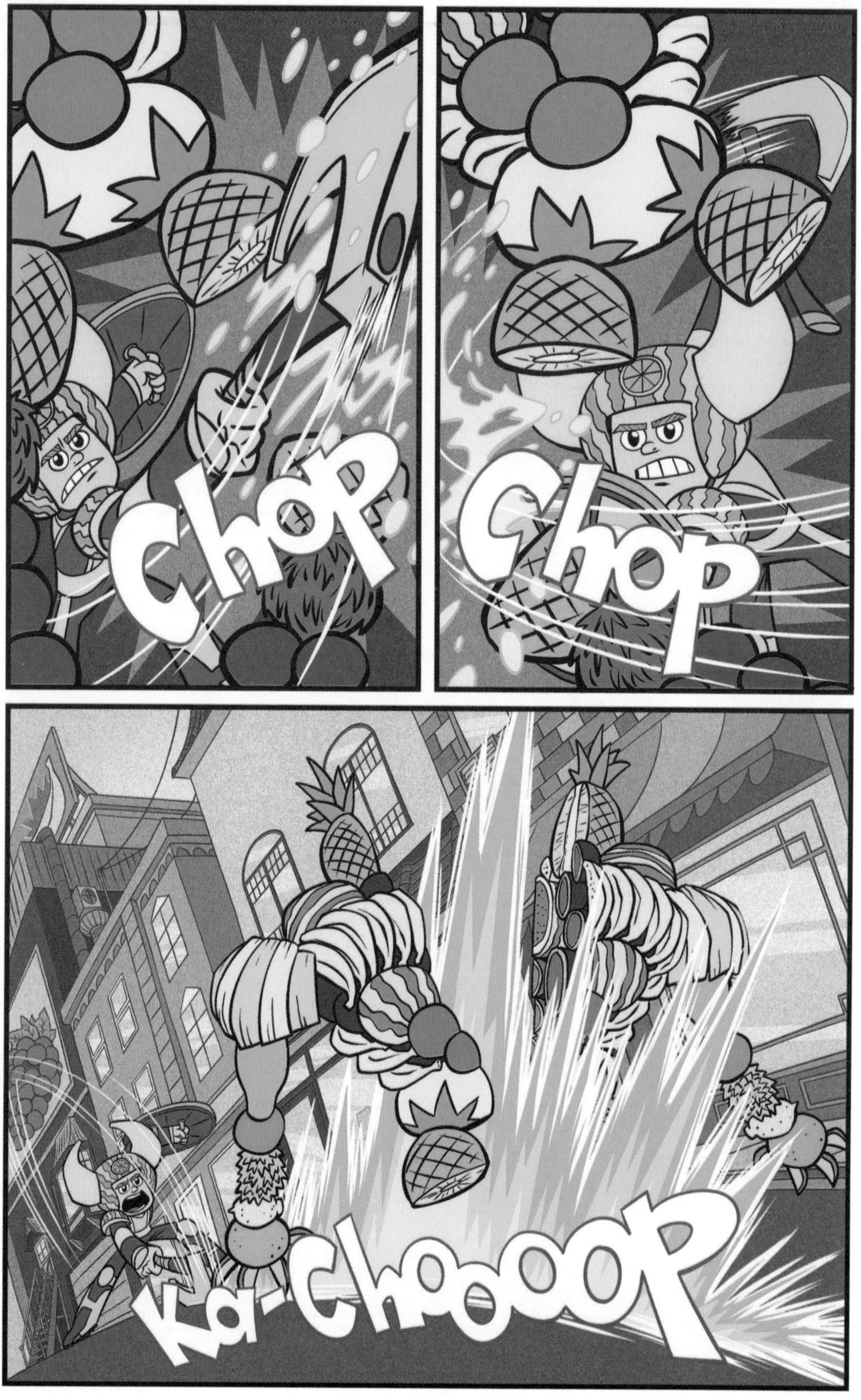
CHOP
CHOP
KA-CHOOOOOP

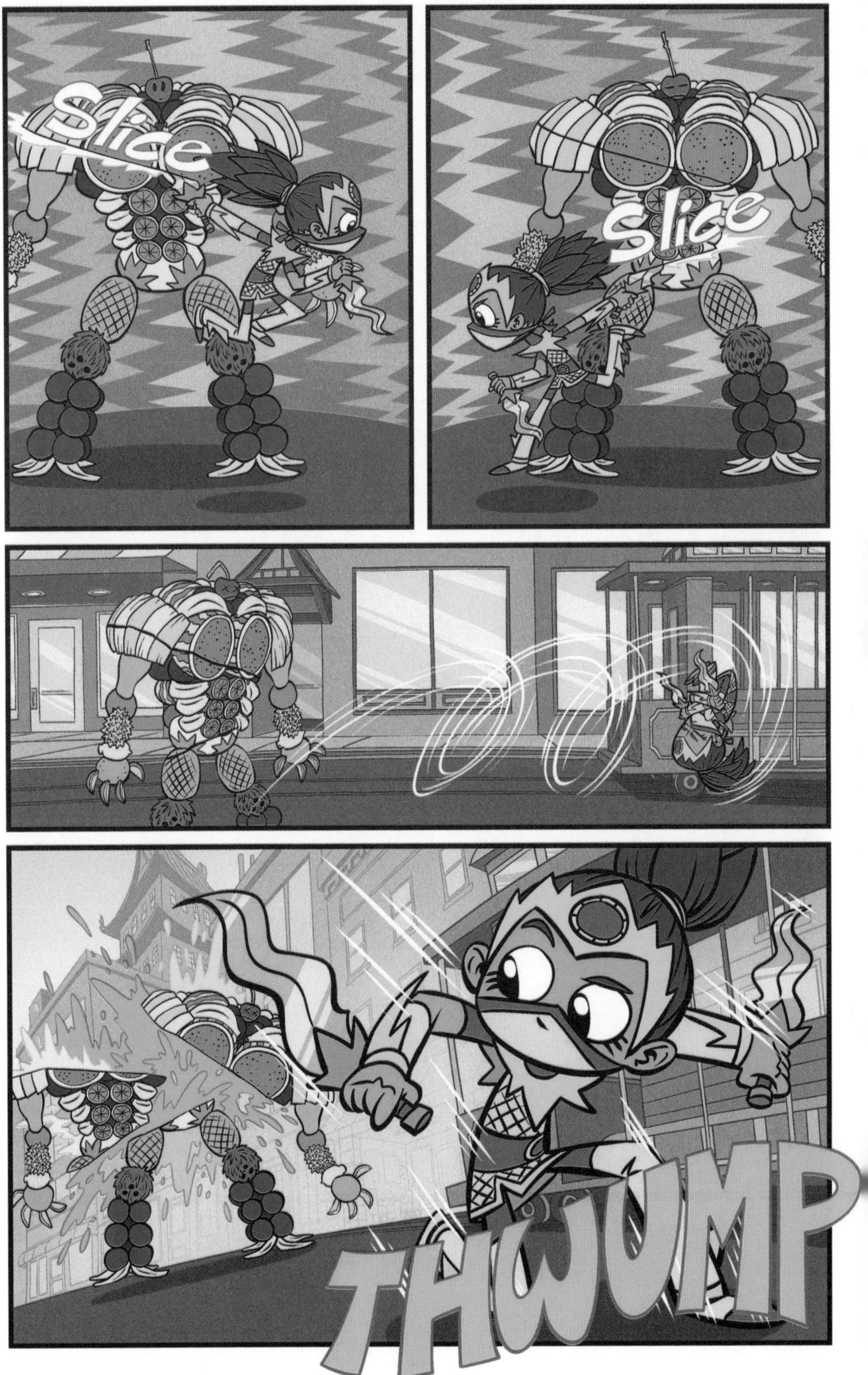
Slice
Slice
THWUMP

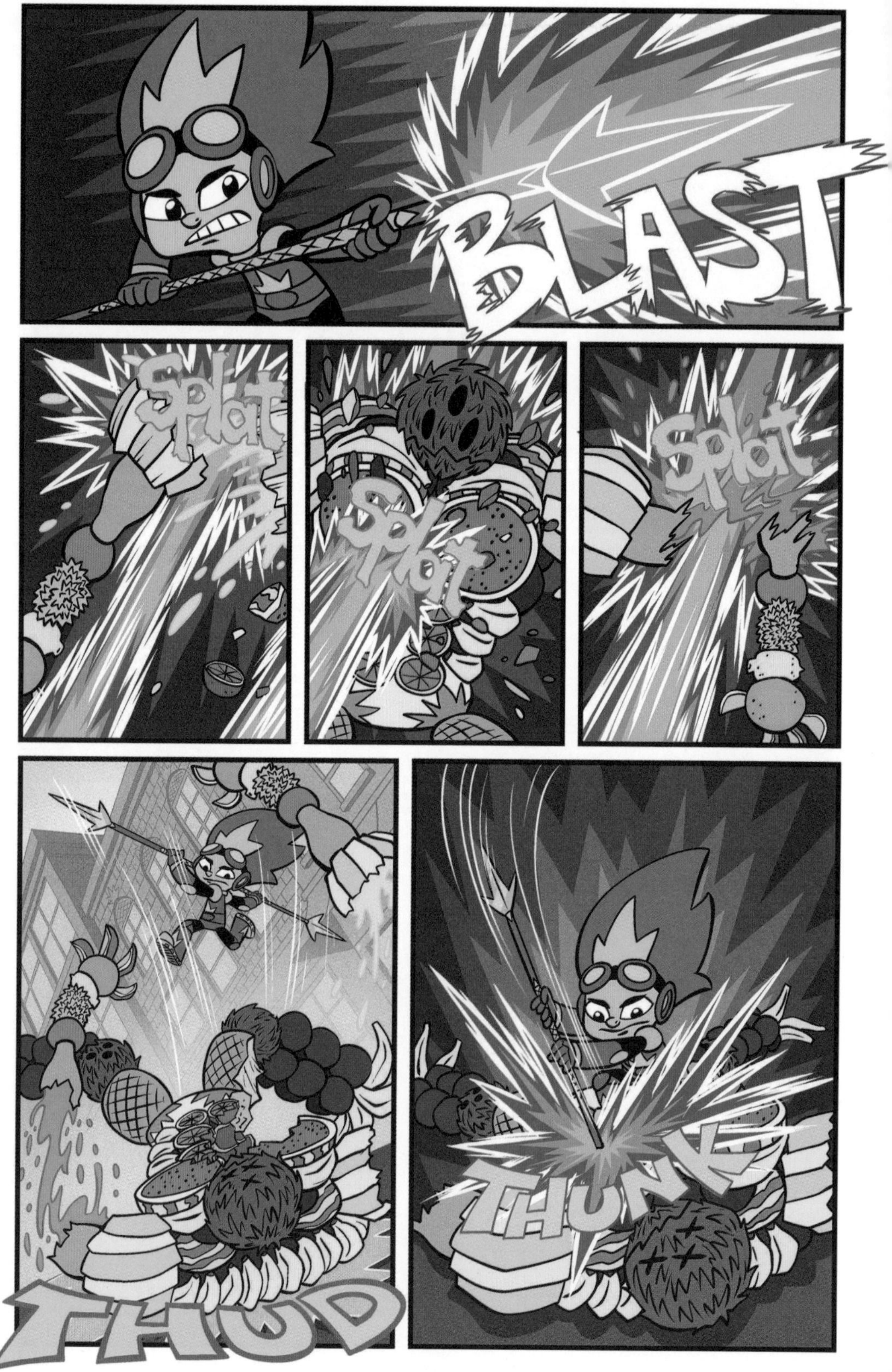
BLAST
Splat
Splat
Splat
THUD
THUNK

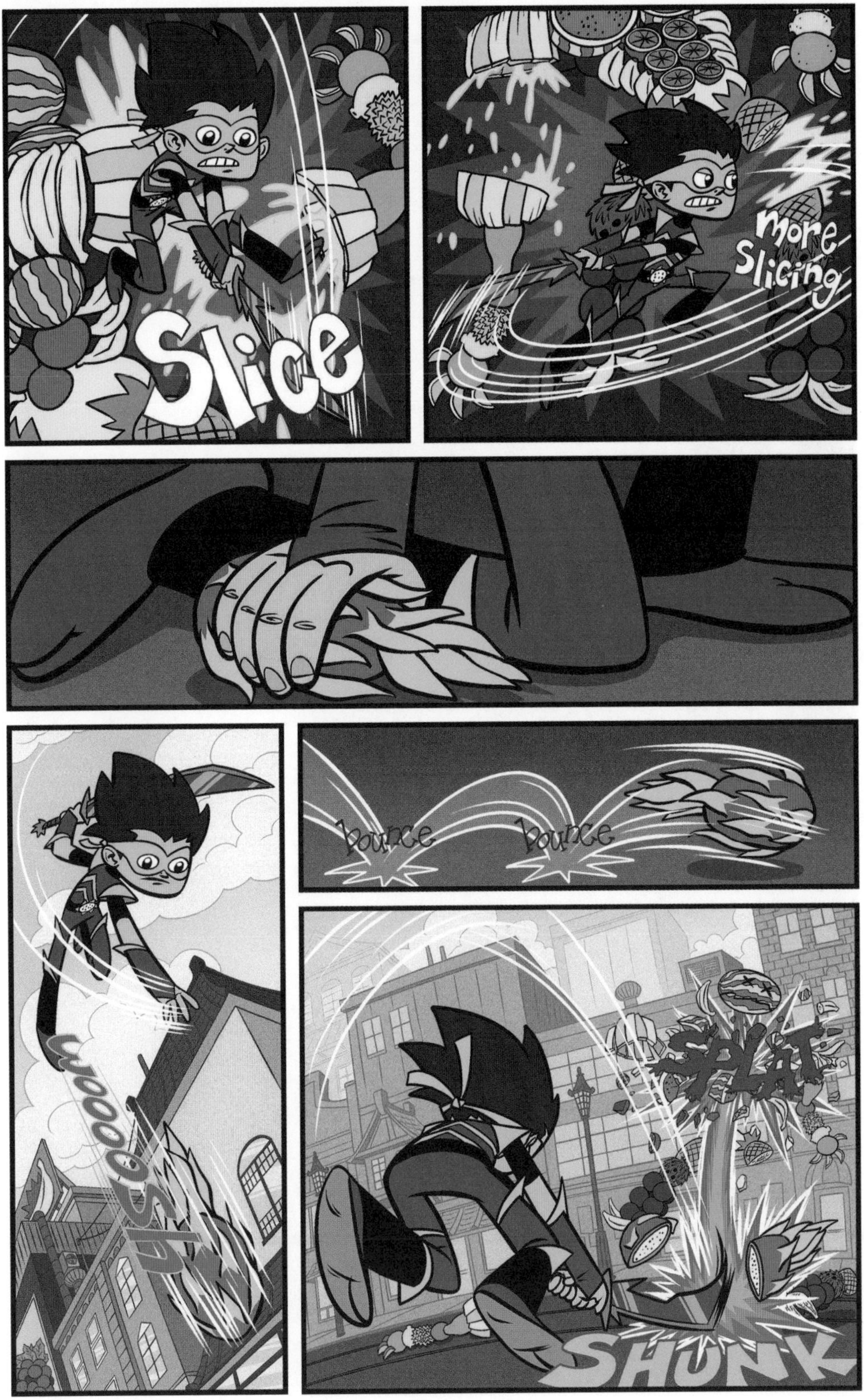
Slice
more Slicing
bounce
bounce
WOOOOSH
SPLAT
SHUNK

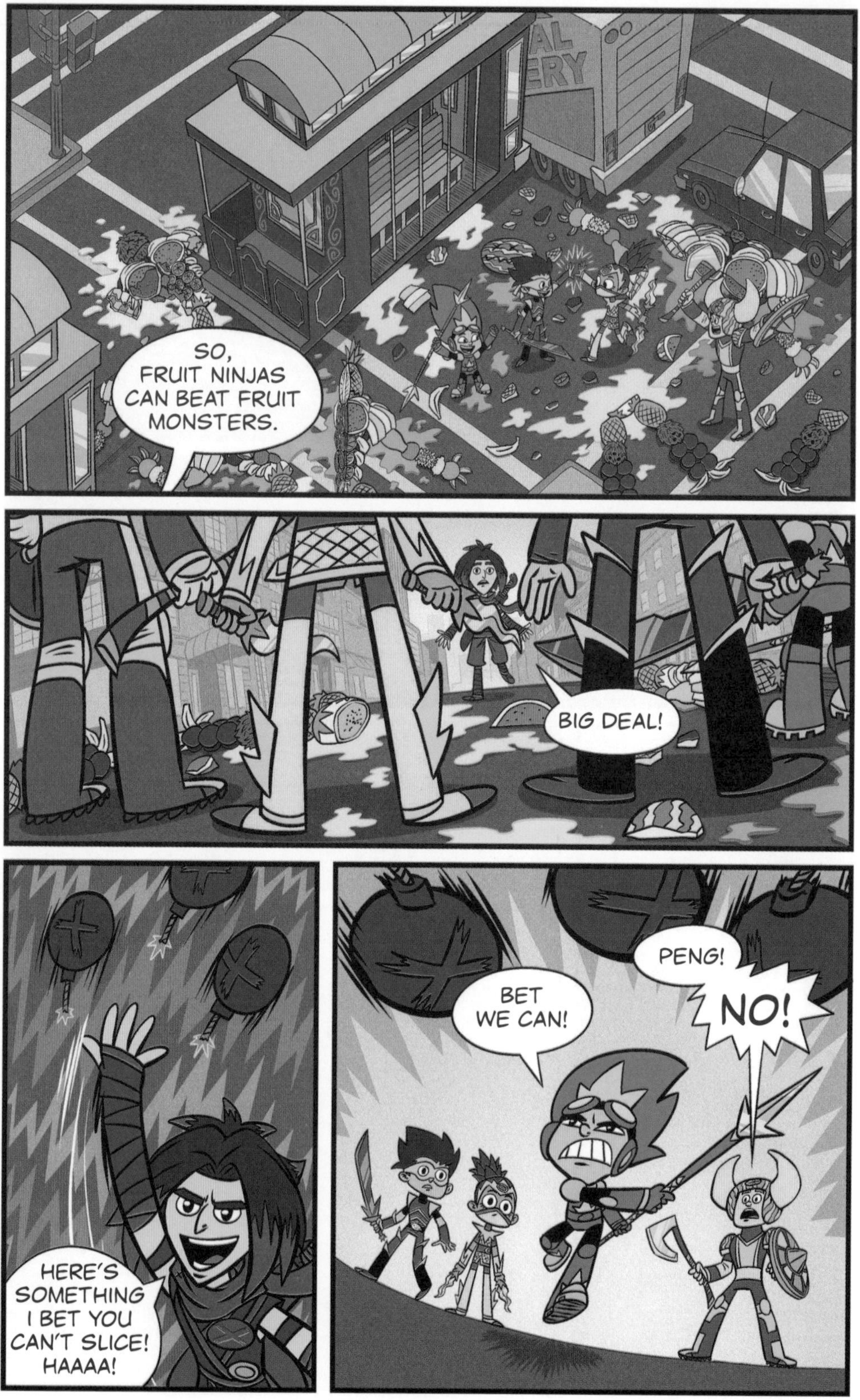
SO, FRUIT NINJAS CAN BEAT FRUIT MONSTERS.
BIG DEAL!
HERE'S SOMETHING I BET YOU CAN'T SLICE! HAAAA!
BET WE CAN!
PENG!
NO!

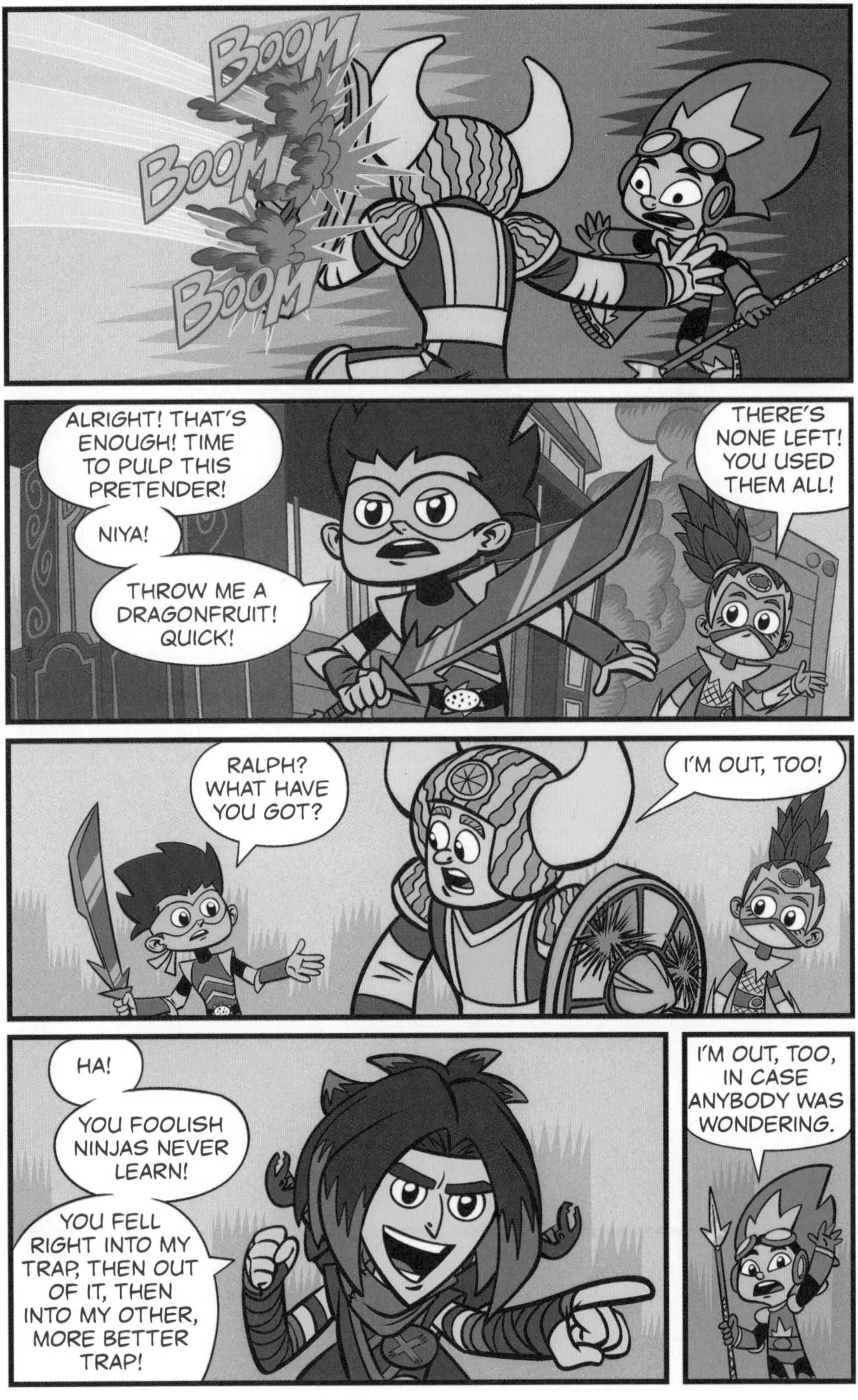
BOOM
BOOM
BOOM
ALRIGHT! THAT'S ENOUGH! TIME TO PULP THIS PRETENDER!
NIYA!
THROW ME A DRAGONFRUIT! QUICK!
THERE'S NONE LEFT! YOU USED THEM ALL!
RALPH? WHAT HAVE YOU GOT?
I'M OUT, TOO!
HA!
YOU FOOLISH NINJAS NEVER LEARN!
YOU FELL RIGHT INTO MY TRAP, THEN OUT OF IT, THEN INTO MY OTHER, MORE BETTER TRAP!
I'M OUT, TOO, IN CASE ANYBODY WAS WONDERING.

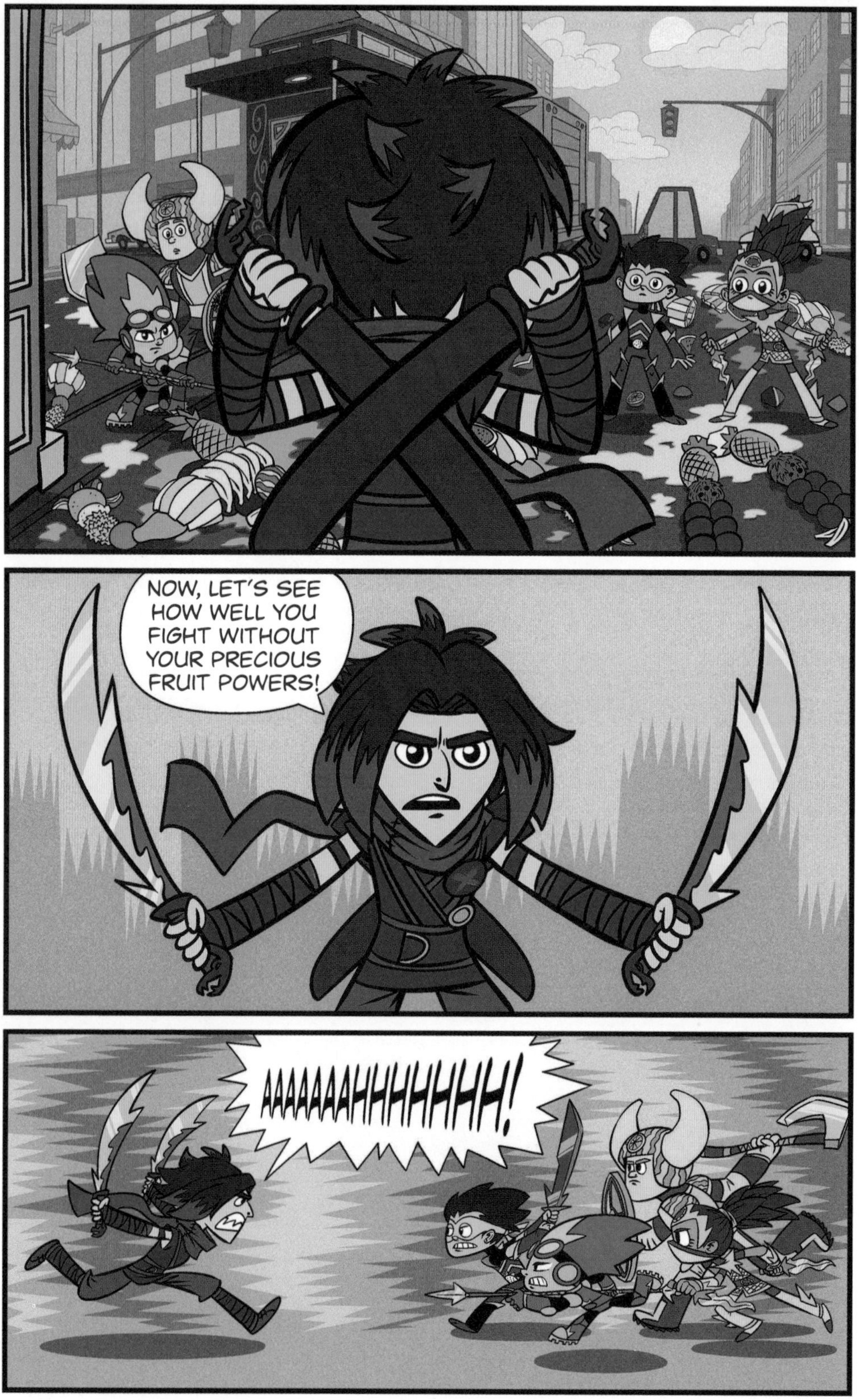
NOW, LET'S SEE HOW WELL YOU FIGHT WITHOUT YOUR PRECIOUS FRUIT POWERS!
AAAAAAAHHHHHHH!

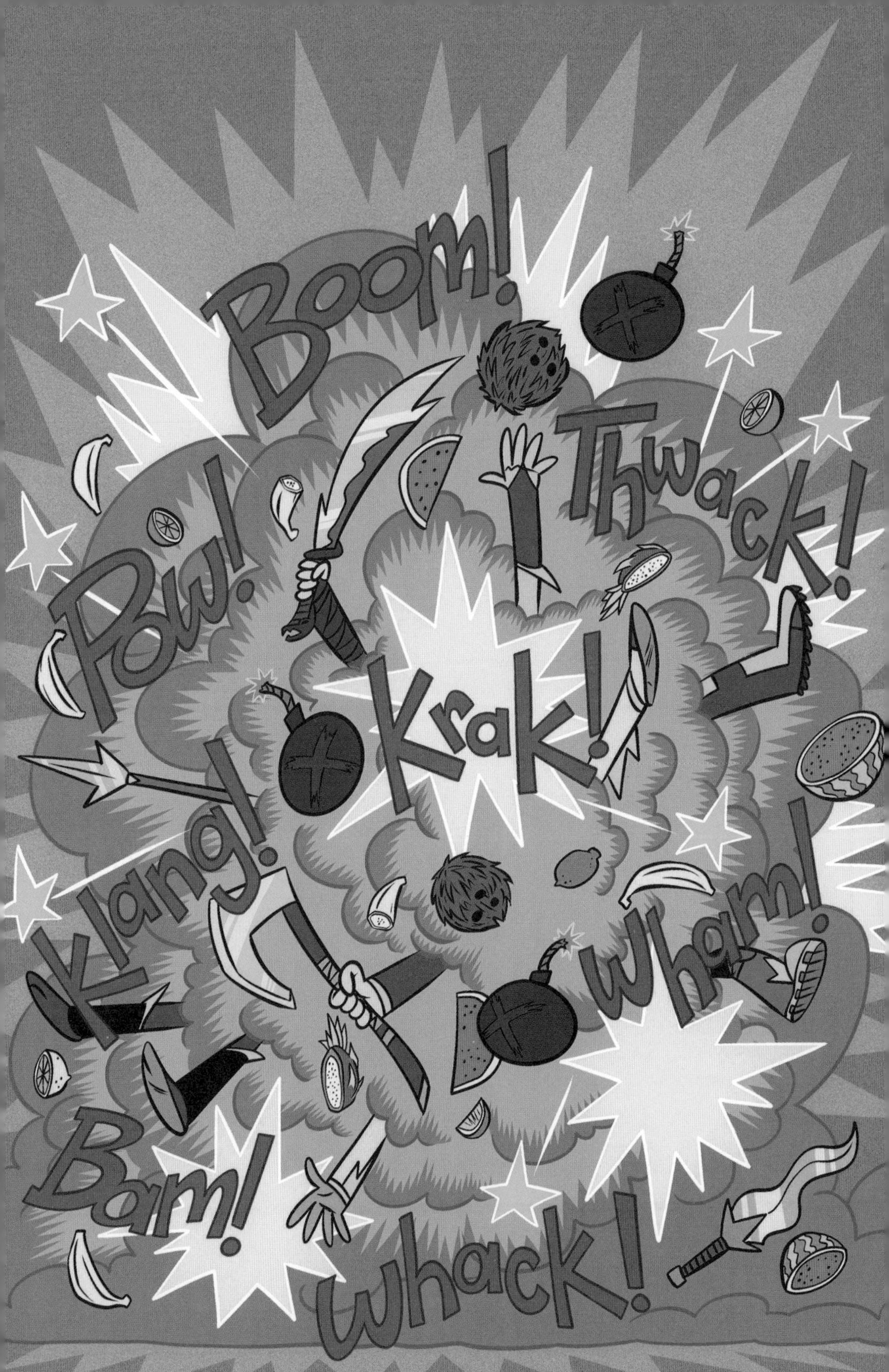
Boom!
Thwack!
Pow!
Krak!
Klang!
Wham!
Bam!
whack!

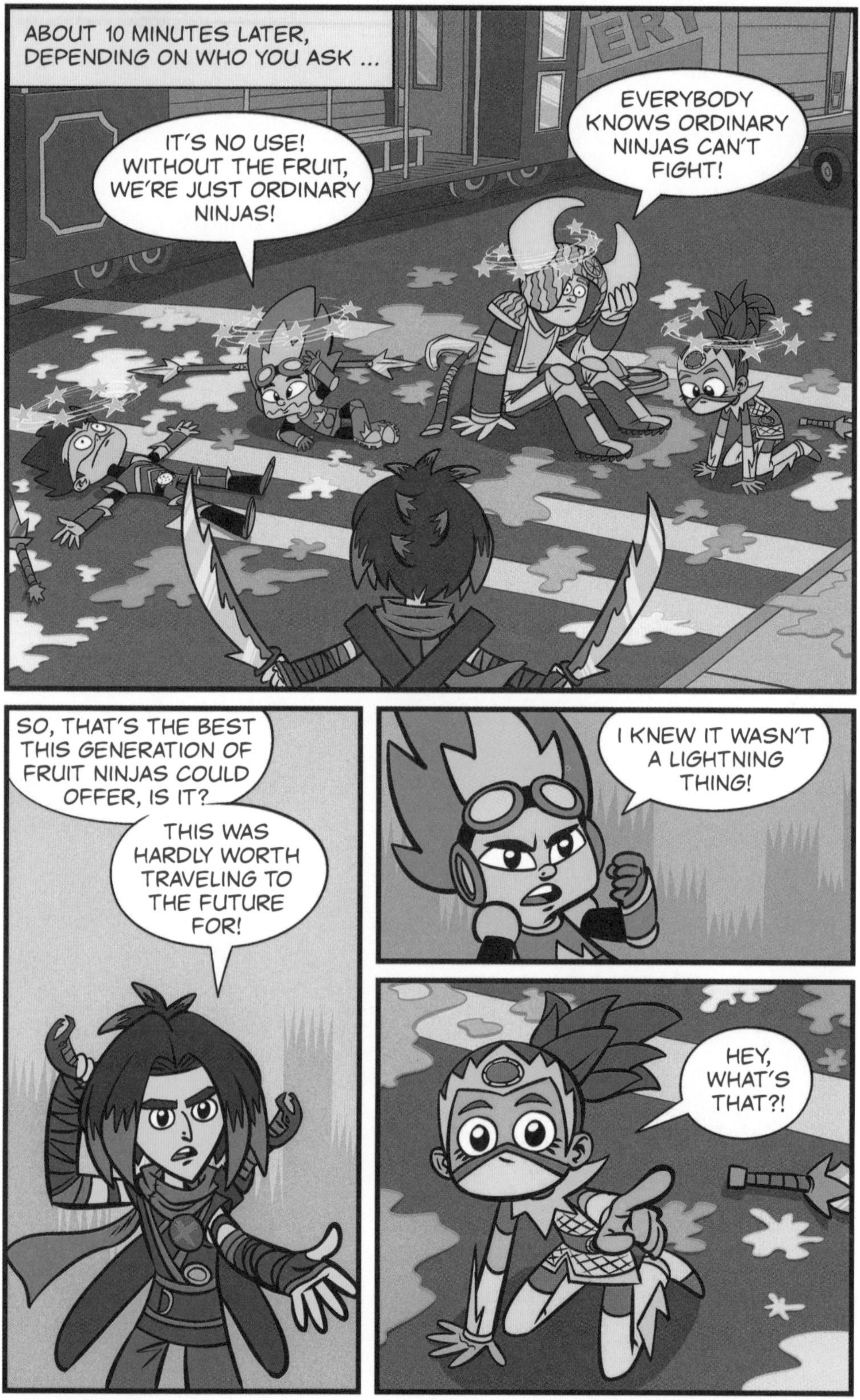
ABOUT 10 MINUTES LATER, DEPENDING ON WHO YOU ASK ...
IT'S NO USE! WITHOUT THE FRUIT, WE'RE JUST ORDINARY NINJAS!
EVERYBODY KNOWS ORDINARY NINJAS CAN'T FIGHT!
SO, THAT'S THE BEST THIS GENERATION OF FRUIT NINJAS COULD OFFER, IS IT?
THIS WAS HARDLY WORTH TRAVELING TO THE FUTURE FOR!
I KNEW IT WASN'T A LIGHTNING THING!
HEY, WHAT'S THAT?!

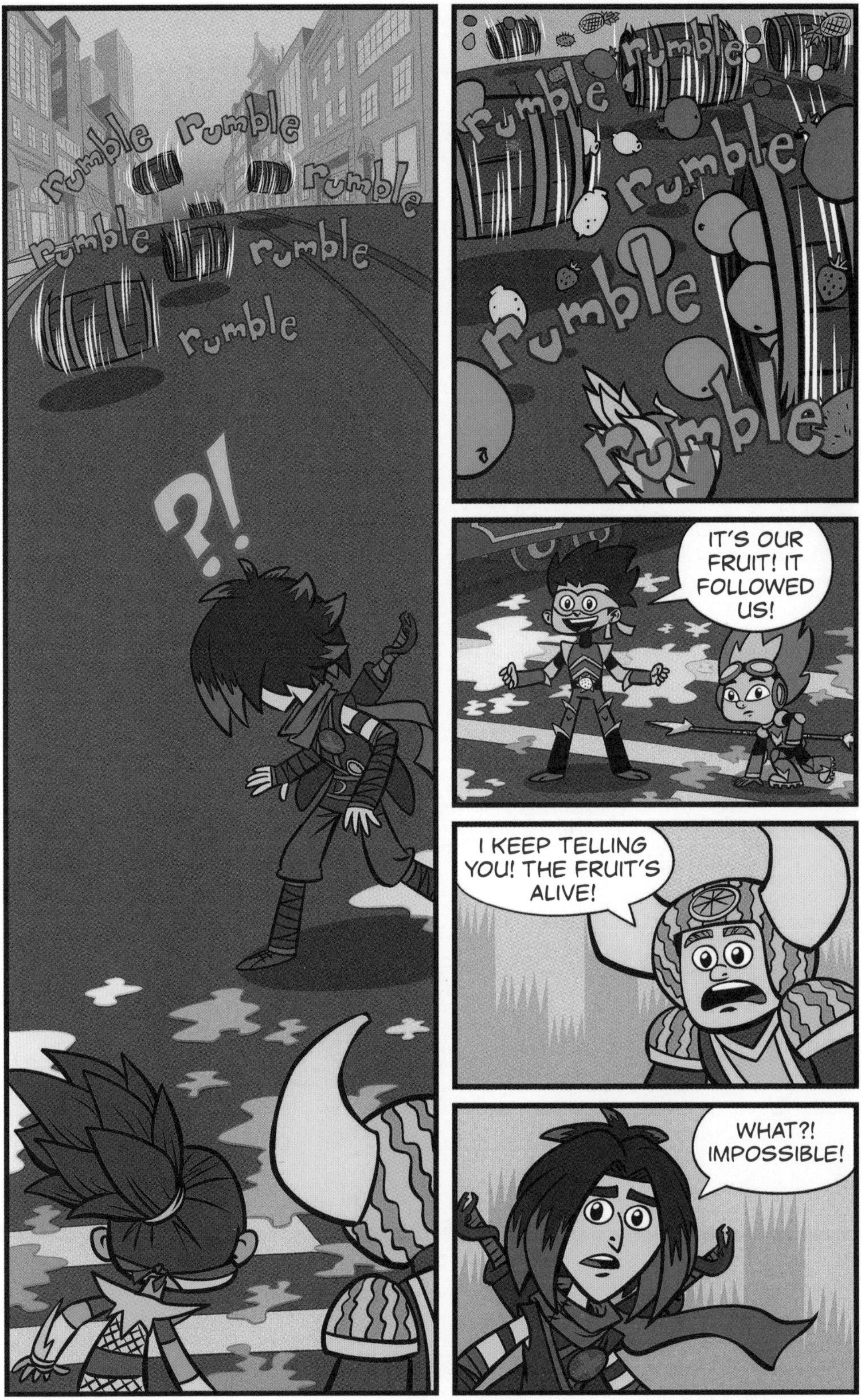
rumble rumble rumble
rumble rumble
rumble
?!
rumble rumble
rumble
rumble
rumble
IT'S OUR FRUIT! IT FOLLOWED US!
I KEEP TELLING YOU! THE FRUIT'S ALIVE!
WHAT?! IMPOSSIBLE!

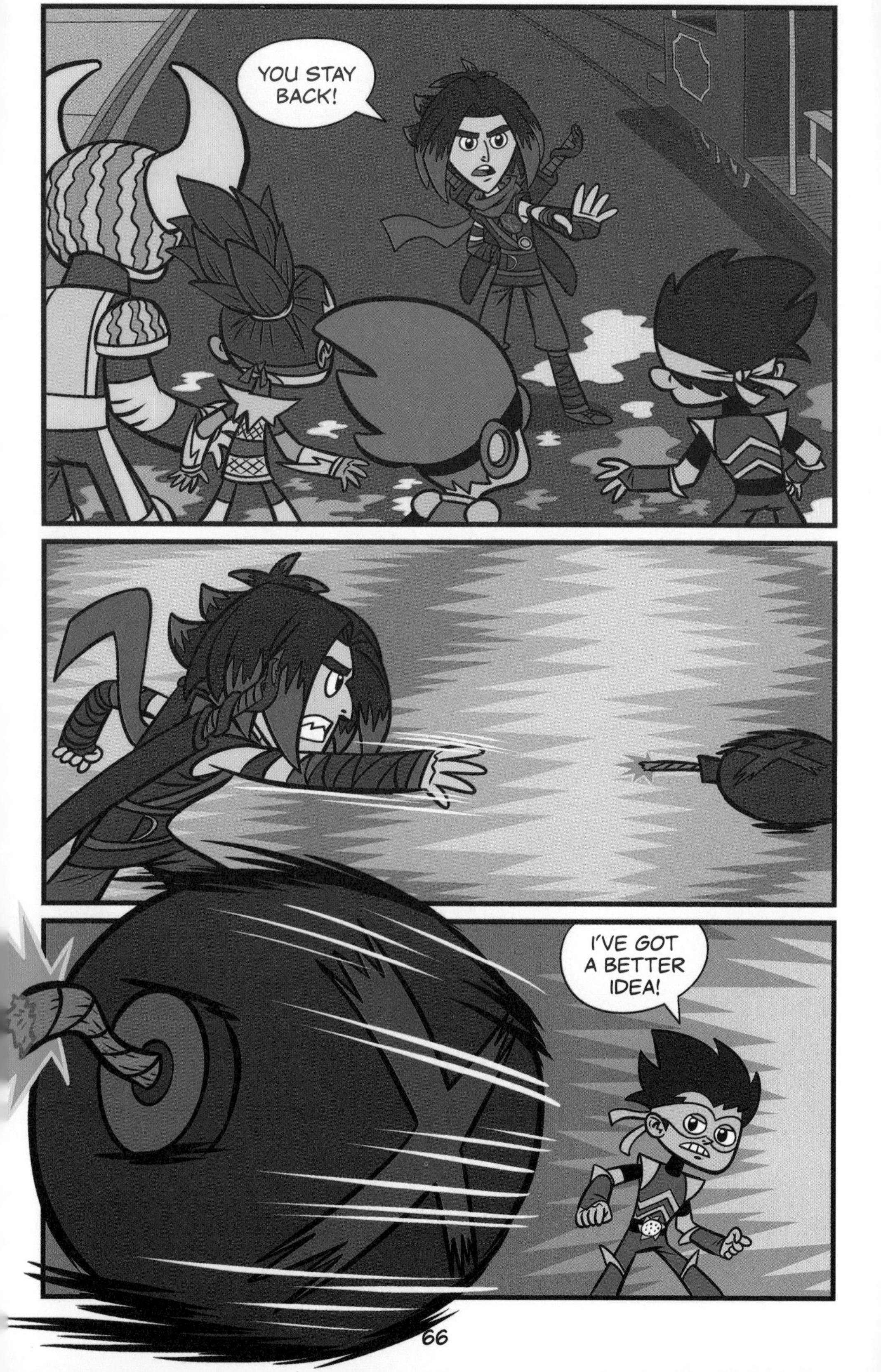
YOU STAY BACK!
I'VE GOT A BETTER IDEA!

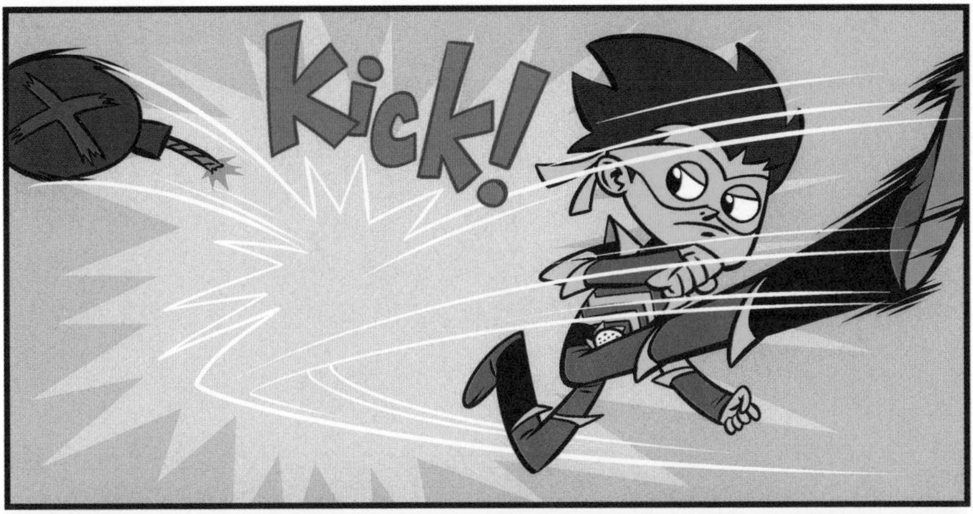
KICK!

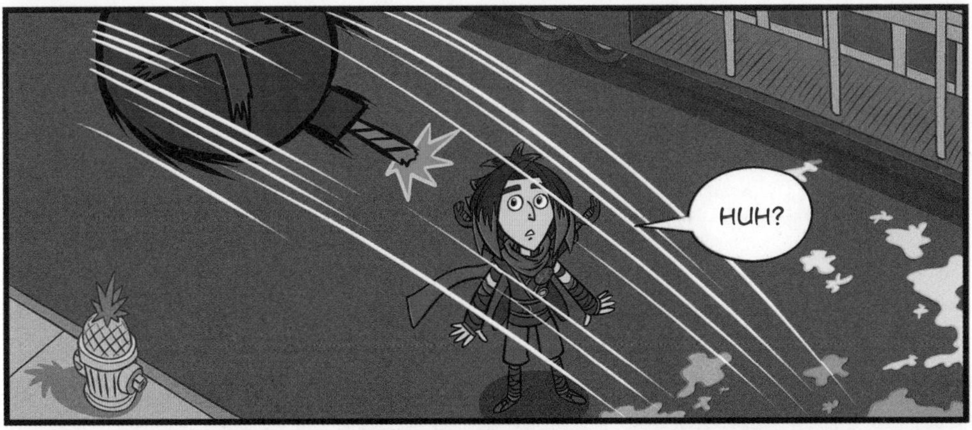
HUH?

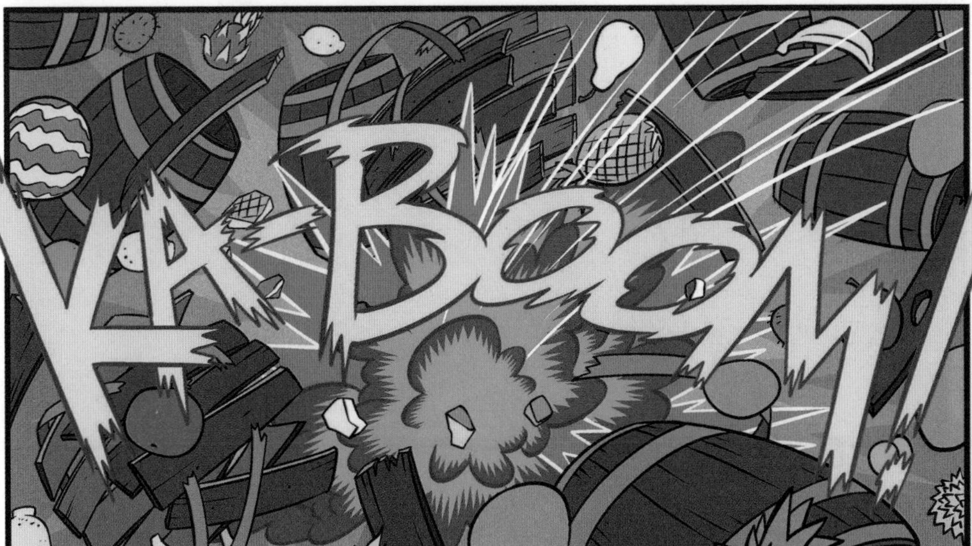
KA-BOOM!

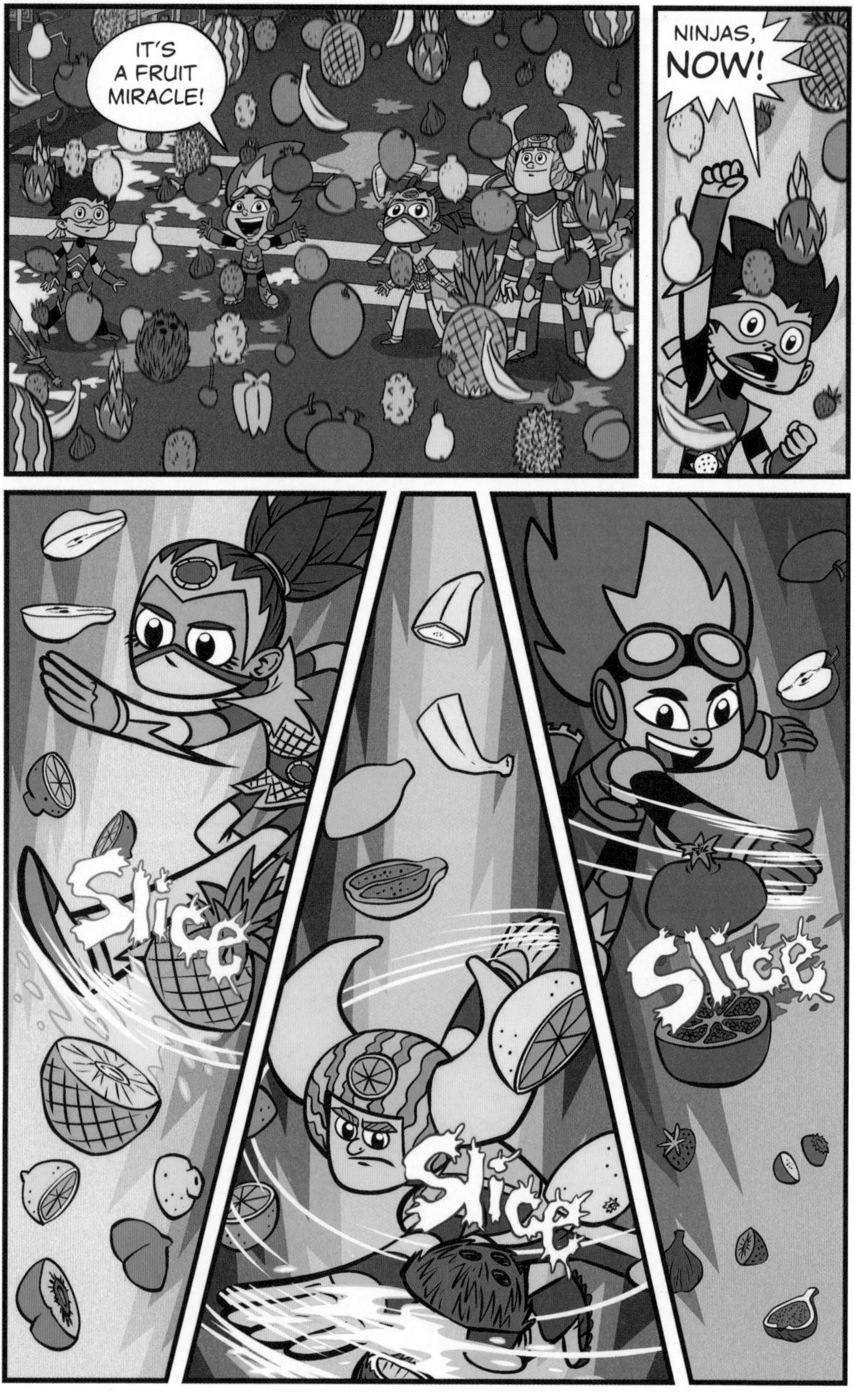
IT'S A FRUIT MIRACLE!
NINJAS, NOW!
Slice
Slice
Slice

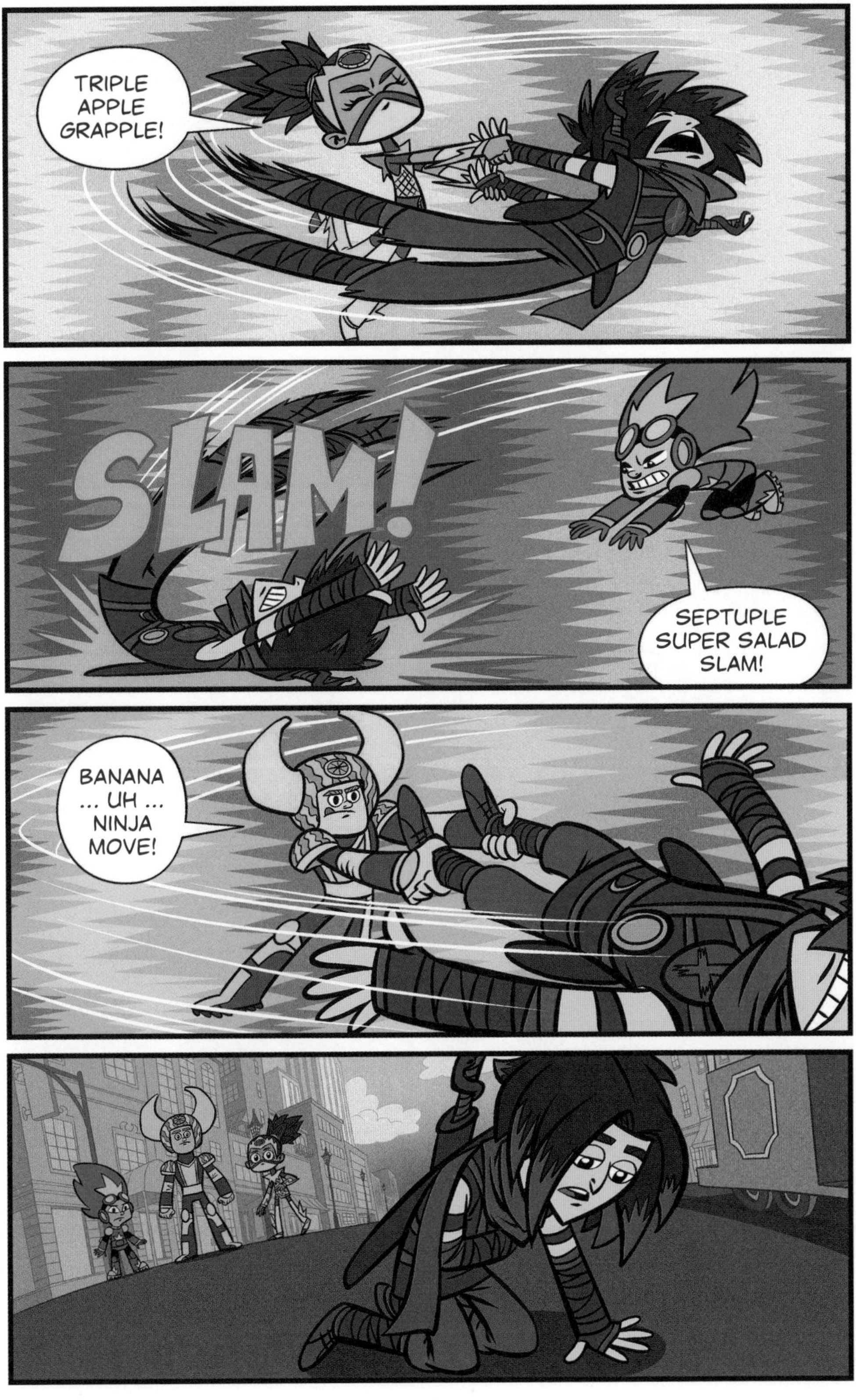
TRIPLE APPLE GRAPPLE!
SLAM!
SEPTUPLE SUPER SALAD SLAM!
BANANA ... UH ... NINJA MOVE!

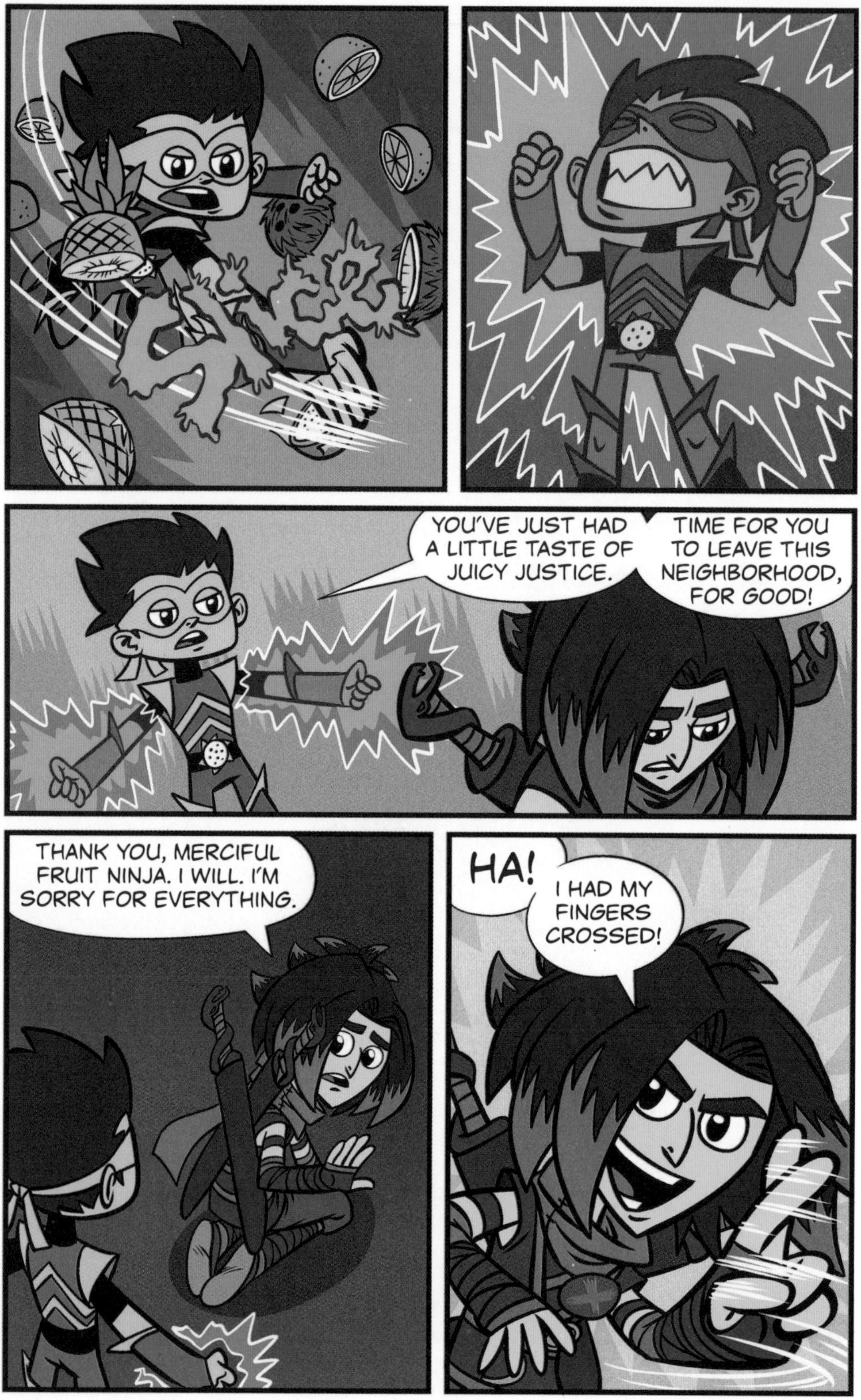
YOU'VE JUST HAD A LITTLE TASTE OF JUICY JUSTICE.
TIME FOR YOU TO LEAVE THIS NEIGHBORHOOD, FOR GOOD!
THANK YOU, MERCIFUL FRUIT NINJA. I WILL. I'M SORRY FOR EVERYTHING.
HA!
I HAD MY FINGERS CROSSED!

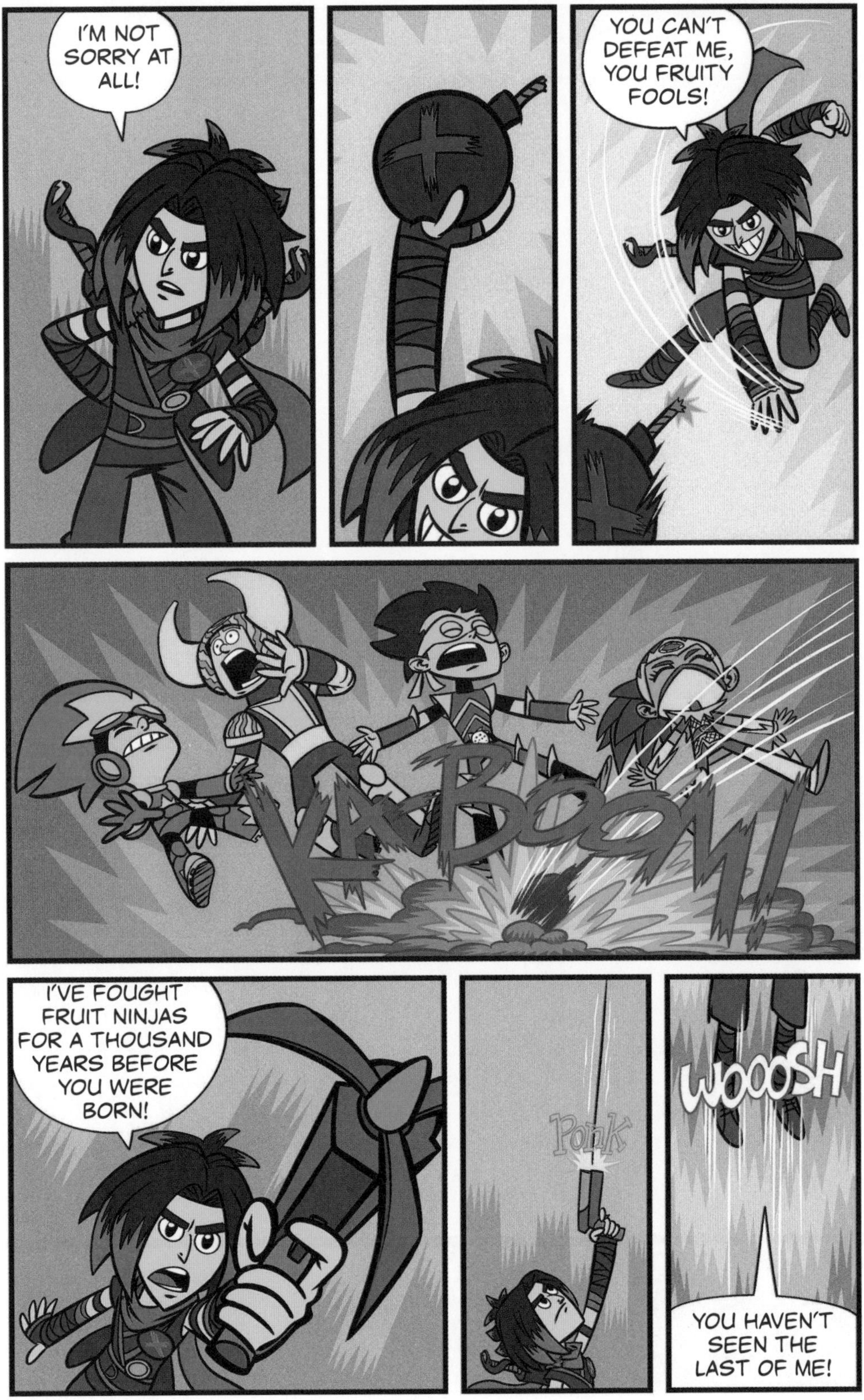
I'M NOT SORRY AT ALL!
YOU CAN'T DEFEAT ME, YOU FRUITY FOOLS!
KA-BOOM!
I'VE FOUGHT FRUIT NINJAS FOR A THOUSAND YEARS BEFORE YOU WERE BORN!
PONK
WOOOSH
YOU HAVEN'T SEEN THE LAST OF ME!

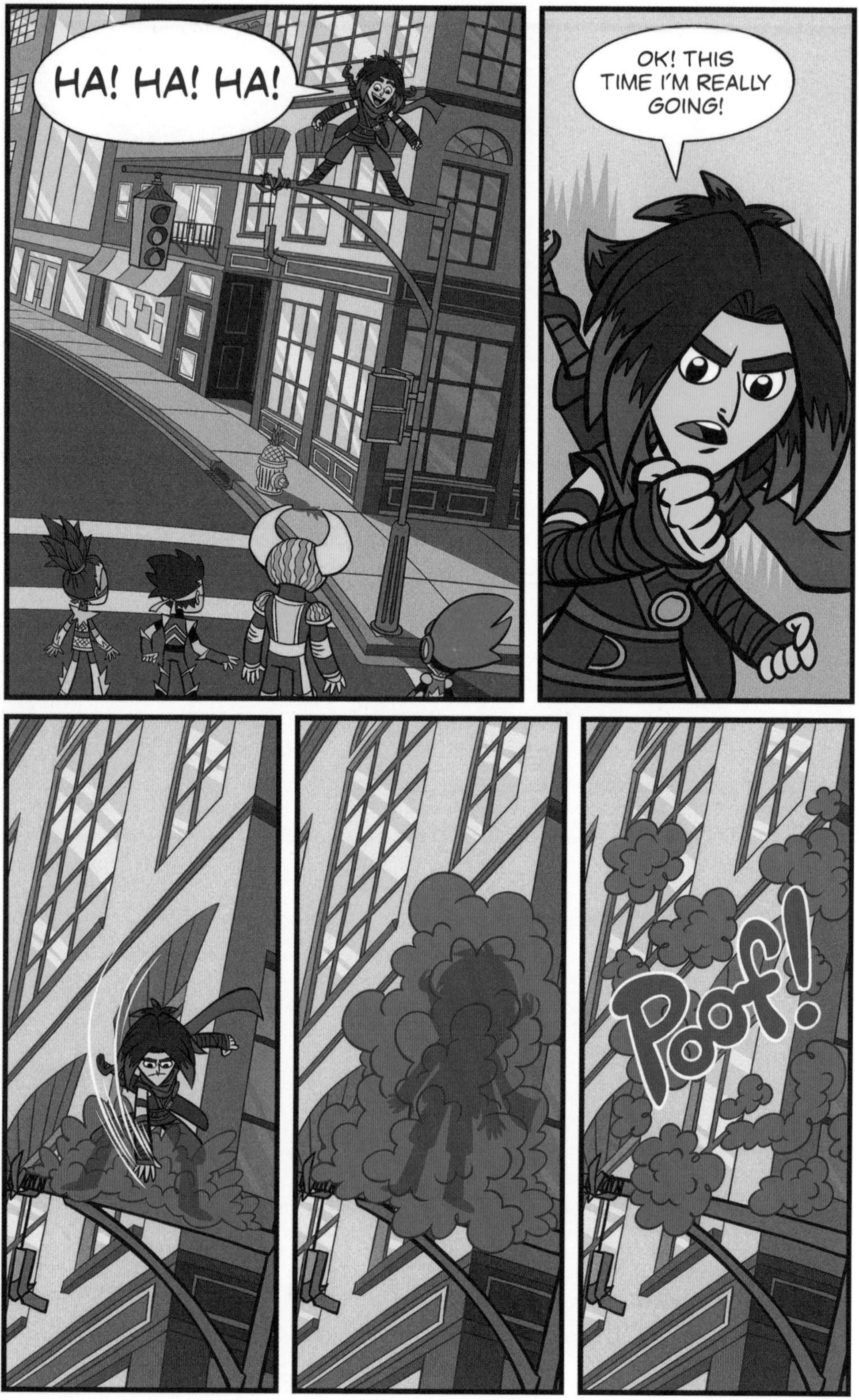
HA! HA! HA!
OK! THIS TIME I'M REALLY GOING!
Poof!

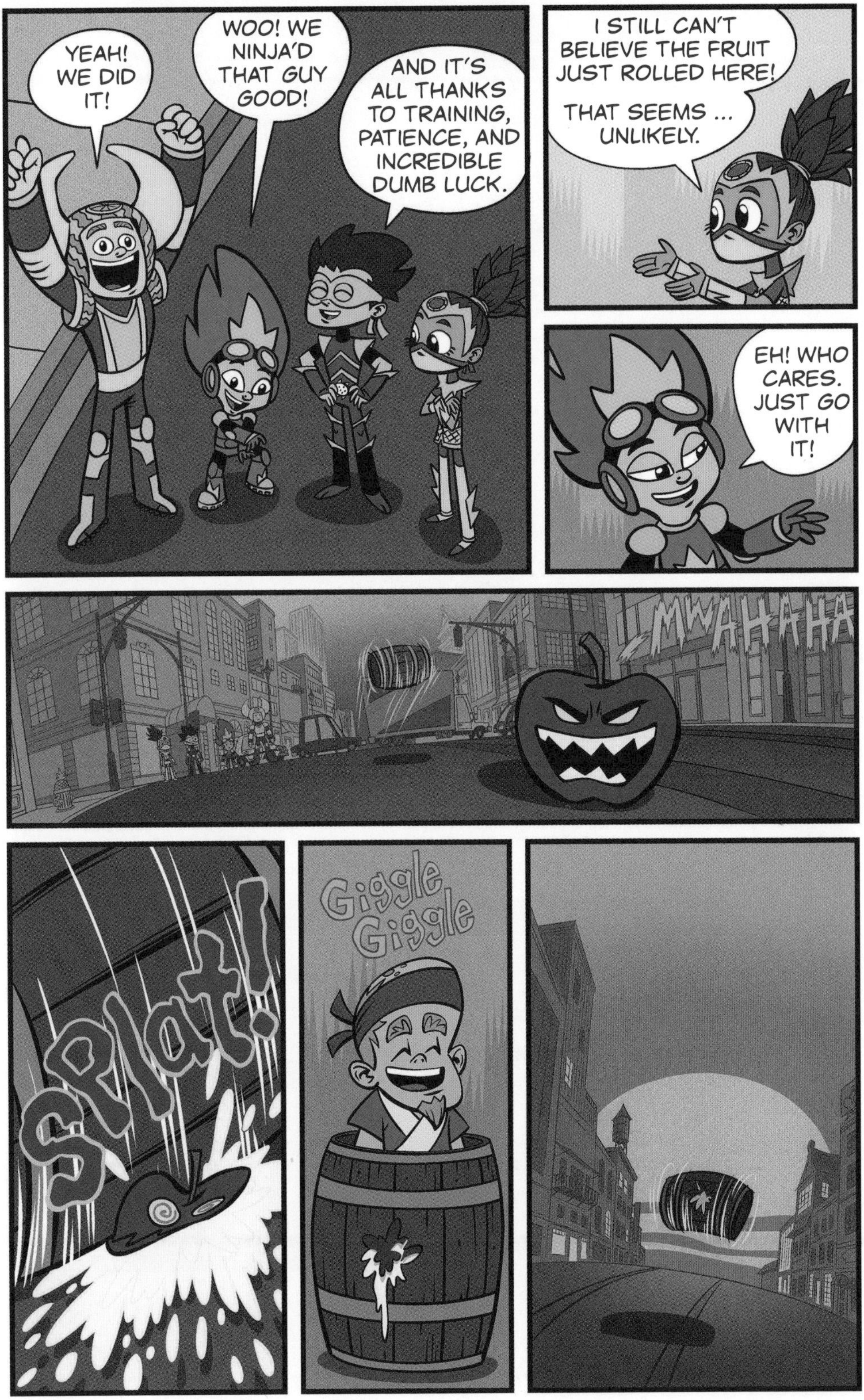
YEAH! WE DID IT!
WOO! WE NINJA'D THAT GUY GOOD!
AND IT'S ALL THANKS TO TRAINING, PATIENCE, AND INCREDIBLE DUMB LUCK.
I STILL CAN'T BELIEVE THE FRUIT JUST ROLLED HERE!
THAT SEEMS ... UNLIKELY.
EH! WHO CARES. JUST GO WITH IT!
MWAHAHA
SPLAT!
Giggle Giggle

SECRET NINJA MESSAGES

Use lemon juice and a paint brush to create secret messages or drawings on white paper. Let them dry overnight. (You won't be able to see the secret message.)

Place the paper under several layers of newspaper. With the help of an adult, lightly iron over the paper with an iron set on high (no steam) until the secret message or artwork appears. Try to guess why the pictures appeared!

Why it works: Lemon juice is acidic and weakens the paper. When exposed to heat, the acidic parts of the paper (your message) burns before the rest of the paper does. It works with milk, too!

FRUIT SMOOTHIE

There are endless flavor combinations for creating your own smoothies at home. You can swap out the fruits listed in the ingredient list for some of your other favorites. Let your taste buds be in control, and have fun!

SERVES 2

INGREDIENTS:

1 cup frozen berries
1 banana
1 cup frozen peaches
½ cup orange juice
1 cup milk

Blend all the ingredients in a blender until smooth. Add more juice or milk for desired consistency. Pour into glasses and enjoy!

FRUIT SMILE

This is a healthy snack that you can't help but smile when making. Everyone will want to eat their fruit now!

With the help of an adult, cut an apple into slices. Smear each piece with peanut butter, and then stick marshmallows on the peanut butter. Top it off with another apple slice and you have a smile even the dentist will be impressed by!

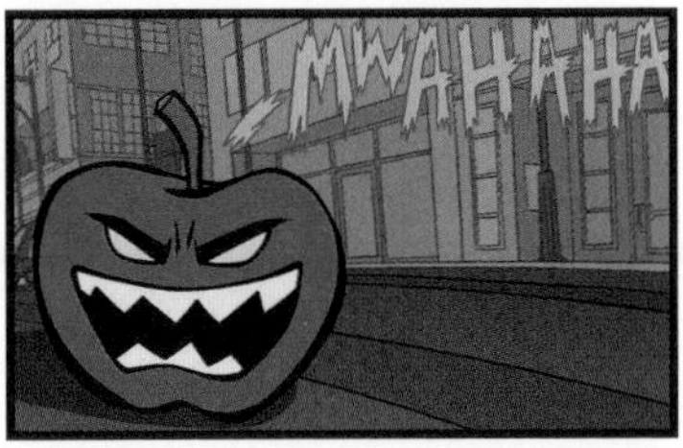
MWAHAHA

FRUITY WORD SEARCH

```
L E E S P E E L B R H G S C
Y N V K K F T F E S Z H H D
Z Q E L P P A R R X B M D W
N F W D E B N U R P U H U T
A J A W G X A I Y T Y I A I
Y U T Y N J R T P U P N K U
F I E P A I G A F N A V P R
B C R D R G E S G O O A Q F
P E M U O F M I I C K N N N
N J E R G K O A M O F A G O
K I L I O G P V X C E N P G
O T O A Q S Q F I R C A T A
V S N N N R E C A M J B I R
R U M K S Y G U A V V Y Q D
```

Durian	Orange	Coconut
Dragonfruit	Juice Jitsu	Berry
Pomegranate	Peel	Banana
Watermelon	Fruitasia	Apple

WHO WERE THE NINJAS?

In 15th-century Japan, ninjas were highly trained secret agents and mercenaries. They specialized in spying, sabotage, infiltration, assassination, and guerrilla warfare. This meant they used their sneaky skills to help defeat the enemies of their masters. According to legend, ninjas had amazing abilities such as invisibility, walking on water, changing into animals, and controlling the elements. In reality, they were masters of disguise and used techniques that helped them escape their enemies and avoid being caught.

THE BIG QUESTION: ARE TOMATOES FRUITS OR VEGETABLES?

Technically speaking, a tomato is a fruit. According to botanists (scientists who study plants), a fruit is the part of the plant that comes from the fertilized ovary of a flower and typically has seeds. A vegetable, on the other hand, is any other part of the plant that you can eat: leaves (like cabbage, lettuce, and spinach), roots (carrots, beets, turnips), stems (asparagus), tubers (potatoes), bulbs (onions), and the flower itself (cauliflower and broccoli).

However, according to the U.S. Supreme Court, a tomato is a vegetable. In 1893, a case came to the court, *Nix v. Hedden*. John Nix was the owner of the largest seller of produce in New York City at the time. His company was one of the first to import produce from Virginia, Florida, and Bermuda to New York. In 1883, President Chester A. Arthur signed a tariff that taxed imported vegetables, but not fruit. Nix sued Edward L. Hedden, collector of the Port of New York, to recover the money he had to pay in taxes. Nix argued that a tomato was a fruit because it has seeds. However, the court ruled that the tomato should be considered a vegetable because of the way it's used (typically served as part of the main meal instead of as a dessert).